WAR GIRL ANNA

WAR GIRLS, BOOK 3

MARION KUMMEROW

CONTENTS

War Girl Anna, War Girls Book 3

Marion Kummerow

Cover Design by http://www.StunningBookCovers.com

Cover Image: Bundesarchiv, Bild 183-S91935 / CC-BY-SA 3.0

https://creativecommons.org/licenses/by-sa/3.0/de/deed.en

READER'S GROUP

Marion's Newsletter

Sign up to my newsletter and download my short story DOWNED OVER GERMANY for free.

It tells you the story of Tom Westlake, British RAF Pilot story, before he met one of the Klausen sisters – Ursula – and fell in love with her.

http://kummerow.info/newsletter-2

CHAPTER 1

January 1944, Ravensbrück Germany

Anna buttoned up her blouse, her body aching and her soul weeping. She didn't dare look at her tormenter – the man who'd viciously violated her, time and again. The sight of his smug expression made her itch to wring his neck with her cold, bare hands and watch his useless life slip from his body. Either that, or vomit all over him.

In her mind she called him T the devil. Every single unfortunate soul in the camp would agree with her verdict that he was the devil incarnate. Doctor Tretter, head physician at the Ravensbrück women's concentration camp, liked to inflict pain and horror. And he did it with a smile.

Sobs threatened to bubble up, but she swallowed them down. Like she always did when the sheer horror of what her life had become threatened to overwhelm her. She'd struck a bargain with the devil.

And she'd gotten the short end of it. But then again, it really wasn't a deal at all.

Her body at his beck and call in exchange for her sister's life.

She summoned the gaunt face of her beloved baby sister Lotte and her emaciated body, skin stretched over protruding bones, and suppressed a sigh. It had been the right thing to do. Lotte wouldn't have survived the horrors of being a concentration camp inmate much longer. No matter how horrid Anna felt right now, she knew she would make the same bargain again if it meant saving her sister.

Anna would find a way to rescue herself from the clutches of T. One day.

"Nurse Anna," Doctor Tretter's nasal voice sent a shiver down her spine. *He was finished, wasn't he?*

"Yes, Doctor Tretter?" she said with a weary voice, turning around to face him, because she knew he disliked her not looking into his eyes when he gave her a command. She held his gaze and blanked her obvious hatred for him from her eyes.

His lips curled up. "You look beautiful, Nurse Anna."

"Thank you," she managed to say with a subdued voice, casting her eyes downward as if the compliment delighted her.

"You will be the perfect escort for my evening event this coming weekend." A viselike grip squeezed her heart tight. So far, he'd been adamant in hiding their *relationship*. Keeping the sordid details of his regular rape of one of his nurses sealed under lock and key. Anna's cheeks flamed hot at the thought of everyone believing that she actually *liked* this monster, that her constant capitulation to the head physician of Ravensbrück happened by choice.

"With your perfectly straight blond hair, flawless light complexion, and..." Doctor Tretter took a step towards her and put a finger beneath her chin, which caused her eyes to flutter closed in disgust. "Haven't I told you to look at me when I talk to you?" His other hand landed on her cheek with a stinging slap.

"Of course you have. I'm sorry, Doctor Tretter. It won't happen again."

"Good. Because as I said, you will be my escort for the soirée at Professor Scherer's house. Do your best to look pleasing and make sure I am not disappointed in your behavior."

All blood rushed from Anna's face. Professor Scherer was one of the most renowned scientists in the Reich, a man even Hitler consulted. The head of the medicine and human genetics studies carried out at the prestigious University Clinic Charité in Berlin. His one-of-a-kind human biology work catapulted his research light-years ahead of everyone else's. She'd followed his work since the moment she had decided to become a biologist one day. Under any other circumstances she would have given her right arm to meet him, but with T the devil by her side?

She shivered.

"You said...you said you didn't want anyone to know about our...arrangement." Anna's voice stumbled.

He looked at her and then smirked. "And nobody will find out. I have a reputation to protect." His beady eyes roved her body from head to toe as if she were a pesky insect he wanted to stomp on. "What they will see is a grateful nurse who loves spending time with the doctor she so admires for the greatness of his work."

"You expect me..." Anna felt the bile crawl back up and she took some shallow breaths, hoping he wouldn't notice her rising panic. "...to tell everyone how much I admire your work?" Work that comprised torturing innocent prisoners with sadistic medical experiments.

"Exactly. I am applying for a professorship at the Charité, and Professor Scherer's esteem of my person and my scientific research is of the utmost importance. You will gush about my work or face the consequences," he said with a cruel smile.

Anna knew the consequences all too well. Execution. Or worse, becoming a prisoner in the camp where she worked as nurse. Every day she saw with her own eyes what that fate entailed.

"I will not disappoint you," she said and turned to leave.

"Wait," came his sharp voice the moment she put her hand on the door handle. She obediently turned and stared into his grayish-blue eyes. Eyes she longed to scratch out of his face. "Take this, and buy a dress to impress. I don't want to be seen with you in that dull nurse's uniform." He tossed a few clothing ration cards in her direction.

"Thank you," Anna pressed through tightened lips and bent down to pick them up. She'd just stooped even lower, accepting payment for her *services*.

Anna clenched her hands into fists as she fled his apartment, running like crazy until she stumbled across the threshold to her own solitary room in the nurses' dormitory.

CHAPTER 2

Anna undressed and scrubbed her entire body with a wet cloth at the sink in the kitchenette of her room, as if rubbing her skin raw could eradicate T the devil from her life and her memory.

She wished she could take a real shower and cleanse herself of Doctor Tretter's lingering stench, but this late at night the communal showers in the dormitory were already closed.

She hated Doctor Tretter with every fiber of her being, but there was at least one thing she had to give him credit for: he always took precautions not to impregnate her. Probably not out of consideration for her, but to avoid the scandal for him. Just the thought of bearing the devil's child sucked all the energy from her bones, and she had to hold onto the sink in an attempt not to crumple to the floor. Her delicate body convulsed fiercely for several moments before she found her control again.

She slipped into her nightgown and then sank into the

only chair with a cup of hot tea and a heavy sigh. Deliberately shutting her mind down to all unpleasant thoughts, she surveyed the small room she called her own. It had a single bed in the far corner, a small side table with a lamp, an open wardrobe area, and a chest of drawers. A threadbare rug occupied the middle of the space, along with the chair she sat on and a metal tray she used as a makeshift table. The kitchenette consisted of a tiny hotplate, a kettle, and a sink.

Nurses at the camp didn't have need of a real kitchen. Since they were expected to take their meals in the canteen, they didn't even receive ration cards.

Anna wrapped her hands around the hot cup, glancing around the sparsely furnished room and longing for the day when living here would be merely a sad memory. As accommodations went, it was sparse. But each night she returned to it from her horrific work, thinking it was paradise on earth.

A place where she could block out what lay beyond the door. Death. Sickness. Humiliation. Terror. Pain. Where intolerable cruelties had become the norm.

Her glance fell on the phone on her nightstand. Lifting the receiver, she placed a call to her home in Berlin, where her mother and her older sister Ursula lived. Ursula had been the epitome of the *good girl*, never once getting into hot water during her entire childhood and adolescence.

Anna still couldn't fathom how much her sister had changed in the past year. After her husband had died, she – being a prison guard at Plötzensee – had let an escaped British airman run away. *I wonder how he's doing? Is he still alive?*

"Ursula Hermann," her sister answered. Anna's heart jumped with relief at hearing a friendly voice. She pictured Ursula with her long, wavy blonde hair and the sky-blue eyes whose color she shared with Anna and their younger brother, Richard.

"It's me," Anna said, hesitating for a moment, tears pooling in her eyes. "How are you?"

"Anna, darling, don't ask me how I am...how are you?"

Anna took a shuddery breath and then felt the tears begin to roll down her cheeks. "I...I've been better."

"Is...you know...is he still visiting?" Ursula's voice was a mere whisper.

"Almost every day. I don't know how much longer I can take this. I feel so dirty," Anna said with a sob.

"Shh. Anna, isn't there anything you can do?"

"You know, when Elisabeth told me about her job here, I never once believed a word of it. I thought she was exaggerating to make herself more interesting." Anna remembered how Elisabeth had first come to the hospital in Berlin where Anna worked. They'd become friends and Elisabeth had confided to Anna under the pledge of secrecy why she had requested a transfer from Ravensbrück to a normal hospital.

Elisabeth had been lured into becoming a camp nurse by the comparatively stellar pay, and the special perks like extra days off, leather boots, and a warm winter coat – things normal citizens fought hard to obtain. But the sweet girl hadn't been able to stomach the abominable things she'd witnessed in the camp.

"Can't you ask for a transfer like she did?" Ursula asked.

"And risk T's wrath?" Anna heard a distant roar in the

line and added for good measure, "Besides, I'm thankful for the opportunity to learn as much as I can while helping the Reich to rid herself of our enemies."

"I can sympathize." Ursula picked up on Anna's code. "My work at Plötzensee prison is so important for the war effort. I wish I could do more to help. But some days I feel overwhelmed." Ursula's voice conveyed so much misery that Anna felt guilty for burdening her sister with her own problems.

"How is Mutter?" Anna changed the topic, drying the remainder of her tears.

"Despondent. She's all but given up hope for Richard. Since the news that his unit was annihilated in Minsk, there's been no further word. Neither to confirm his death, nor that he's still alive."

"Did you tell her about T…?" Anna asked.

"God forbid, of course not. Do you really think I would tell our mother that…?"

Of course Anna hadn't thought Ursula would bring up such a delicate topic with Mutter, but their mother was very intuitive where her children were concerned. It wouldn't be the first time that she cornered one of her children with assumptions and coerced them into telling the truth.

"She's not asking either," Ursula said, finishing Anna's thought.

"I wish we could give her some good news. Like that the war has ended and Richard and Vater will come home soon."

"Actually, there is good news," Ursula said.

"Tell."

"Aunt Lydia is eligible to receive the Cross of Honor of

8

the German Mother." Aunt Lydia was Mutter's youngest sister. At seventeen, she'd married the son of a farmer and moved with him to rural Bavaria. Since then, almost every year without fail, she'd given birth to another child. The youngest one, a girl called Rosa, was born last fall.

"That is good news for her. It will raise her appreciation amongst the leaders of the district," Anna said carefully. After what happened to Lotte, the entire family had feared repercussions on Lydia and her children. But the fact that her husband – albeit at the front – was well connected and esteemed in the farmer's community had saved her.

"Yes. Lydia called Mutter to let her know that she'll be awarded the Second Class Silver Cross for mothers with six or seven children in a formal ceremony planned on Mother's Day this May. She has invited us to visit," Ursula said and gave an almost inaudible sigh.

"Wouldn't it be nice to travel to Upper Bavaria and visit Lydia and our cousins? For me, I could use a few days off from work." *And from T the devil.*

"I was thinking the same. It's much safer in the country with all those bombings going on in Berlin," Ursula said.

"Since when are you so concerned about your safety? Haven't you told me once and again how important your work as a prison guard is?" *And not in the way a wiretapper might think.*

"You are right, Anna. I should keep up my spirits and not fail our country by being disheartened."

Anna almost giggled at the way Ursula formed her sentence. Most phone calls were tapped and it was never a good idea to oppose Führer and Fatherland. The silly mood made her remember that not all was bleak in her life. "Oh, there's another bit of good news. I was invited to a soirée at Professor Scherer's."

"Professor Scherer? Should I know him?" Ursula asked.

Anna sighed. "He's only the most respected scientist Germany has in the areas of medicine and genetics."

"Anna, darling, that's wonderful," Ursula said with a voice that showed she didn't quite get what was so amazing about this invitation. "I love talking to you, sister, but I have to work the night shift and being late is not an option."

"I know. Take care of yourself. Please?"

"I will, and you do the same. Try to ask for a few days off and come to visit. Mutter would be delighted to see you."

"Goodnight." Anna pulled the phone away from her ear and stared at the gray wall, trying not to think about her disgraceful work, or the man who forced himself on her.

CHAPTER 3

Anna stood in front of the mirror, applying mascara to her eyelashes. As she glanced up to appraise her work, the gaunt skull of a woman stared back at her, the sunken black eyes full of accusation. Anna blinked. Once, twice. But the images of emaciated prisoners kept haunting her. *Murderer*, one of the ghosts called out. *Betrayer of humanity*, another one chimed in. *Scum.*

Anna stepped back from the mirror and slipped on the simple but elegant black two-piece suit Doctor Tretter's ration cards had bought her. The pencil skirt ended mid-calf and showed off her beautiful calves in the new pumps with a sturdy two-inch heel. The jacket was tailored, with shoulder pads and peplums, making her waist look impossibly tiny.

She did a turn, and was satisfied with the way the suit fit her like a glove. *Dressed for the occasion! Prostitute!* The images in her head continued to haunt her.

Today had been another repulsive day at work. Anna

had become a nurse to help people, not murder them. Although she technically didn't kill anyone, she was part of the system designed to annihilate large parts of the population. She didn't have the slightest idea why the Nazis even employed nurses in the camps. There was nothing she could do for the prisoners, besides giving them a smile, when nobody was looking, and a day off from work in the hospital ward – with reduced rations.

I never wanted to work here. I had to do this to save Lotte.

At least the gruesome medical experiments had stopped, because T the devil was busy writing his conclusion to the gangrene research he'd done on those poor Polish women. Anna's breath froze in her chest as she remembered the high-pitched, soul-wrenching cries of the condemned prisoners. After a tense shake of her head, she blocked the memories out. There was nothing she could do.

Satisfied with the way she looked, she smoothed her perfectly straight blonde hair one last time, and applied bright red lipstick. Makeup articles were hard to come by these days, but Doctor Tretter's ration cards had not only sufficed for the new suit, but also to buy much-wanted mascara and a red lipstick to replace the ones she'd treasured for years until she'd used up the last morsel of color.

Ursula will be so jealous, she thought, before she shuddered and questioned her own sanity. How could anyone envy a woman who'd become a handmaiden to the Grim Reaper by day and a prostitute by night?

Shame burnt up her face, shimmering through the carefully applied powder makeup. She closed her eyes for a moment, willing away shame and guilt. Tonight she would seize her opportunity to meet – and impress – the man she'd admired since she was a child, dissecting frogs and snails. Professor Scherer.

A glance at the alarm clock on her nightstand told her it was high time to meet Doctor Tretter. He wouldn't be pleased if she was late. Or actually, he would be. During the past weeks she'd learned that he enjoyed the tiniest of her mishaps or objections, because it gave him a reason to punish her. Make her wince. Cry out in pain.

Anna's brain still couldn't fathom how a fellow human could be so cruel. And T the devil wasn't the only one. Most of the guards at the camp derived pleasure from torturing the prisoners, dreaming up new, crueler methods every day. The doctors competed with each other, orchestrating repulsive experiments, ones that more often than not left their patients dead. Hadn't they taken the Hippocratic Oath to help their patients, not harm them?

Doctor Tretter had demanded Anna meet him in front of the building where he lived. After she arrived, he appeared minutes later in his SS dress uniform with his decorations. They walked to the parking lot, where he'd parked his automobile. The car alone was a testament to how much power he held in the regime. Since the government had seized most private vehicles to be used for the war effort, private citizens no longer owned vehicles of any kind and resorted to bicycles, walking, or public transportation.

Half an hour later, T the devil stopped his car in front of a magnificent castle-like building. Uniformed men approached the automobile and opened the doors. Doctor Tretter showed his identification and then handed over the keys before walking around and clasping Anna's arm tightly above the elbow. He guided her up the impressive flight of stairs, flanked by Roman statues made of white marble. *Does he think I would run away? Where would I go?*

At the front entrance, a liveried butler greeted them, inspecting their invitation and then guiding them to the big salon. All troubling thoughts faded away as Anna surveyed the magnificence spread out before her. She'd never seen such splendor. Sparkling chandeliers, long case clocks with shiny golden frames, and paintings by old masters adorned the entrance hall.

Her breath caught in her throat as she admired every single piece of tasteful decoration. While the mansion reeked of wealth, it wasn't obnoxious or overdone. The big salon was exactly what the name indicated: big. An immense, sparkling chandelier hung from the high ceiling, casting a shimmering light onto the beautiful wooden furniture.

Most of the important-looking men wore highly decorated dress uniforms, and the small minority of civilians wore tuxedos. The women wore evening gowns that made her own two-piece suit look like one of Cinderella's pinafores. Momentarily bedazzled by the sparkling fabrics, elegant hairdos and, carefully applied makeup, Anna had the sudden urge to flee this place.

Doctor Tretter approached a group of people and joined their discussion after the usual greetings and Heil Hitlers. Anna felt a blush stain her cheeks as she realized he had chosen not to introduce her to anyone, effectively letting them know she was not important.

Anna ignored the nasty feeling creeping up her spine, but held her head high and her shoulders straight. With nothing else to do, she followed Doctor Tretter like a shadow, stopping when he did, and unobtrusively listening to the conversations going on around her.

"There is Professor Scherer." Doctor Tretter grabbed Anna's arm again and hissed, "You'd better do your best to charm him. It's very important to my career that I make a good impression on him this evening."

She wanted to refuse, for the sole purpose of diminishing T the devil's chances for the coveted professorship at the Charité, even if that meant she'd burn at the stake for her insolence. But when she spied the handsome man in his fifties, she forgot how much she despised Doctor Tretter and saw only the professor whose work she'd admired for more than a decade.

Anna had always aspired to become a renowned biologist. And if it weren't for the war, she'd have found a way to convince her parents to support her dreams. Anna burnt with ambition. One day she would claw her way into university, and work hard enough to achieve a career most men could only dream of. *I will make an impression on him, all right.*

CHAPTER 4

Doctor Tretter approached the professor, pasting a confident smile upon his face, looking every bit like the competent and skilled research doctor.

"Professor Scherer, it's always a pleasure to see you," Doctor Tretter said, clicking his heels and raising his hand in the *Hitlergruß*.

"Doctor Tretter, the pleasure is all mine," Professor Scherer answered. Anna groaned inwardly, at T the devil's *oversight* in not mentioning her name.

"There are so many things I'd like to discuss with you about my latest discoveries on the gangrene bacteria–" Tretter stopped mid-sentence when the professor turned toward Anna.

"I'm afraid we weren't introduced, Fräulein?" he asked, looking her straight in the eye. As if she mattered.

"This is Nurse Anna. She works for me." Tretter all but growled at the professor. As Anna considered his words, she noted that T the devil's tone and insolence were ruining his image far more than she could ever do.

"I'm delighted to make your acquaintance, Fräulein..."

"Klausen, Anna Klausen," Anna said.

"Fräulein Klausen. Welcome to my home." The professor reached out his hand and when she dutifully placed her fingers in it, he gracefully lifted them to his lips and blew a kiss on the back of her hand.

Anna was more than a little impressed by Professor Scherer. She'd admired his work for so many years that she could hardly believe she was meeting her idol in person. One of the few men in attendance wearing a tuxedo, he exuded the distinguished aura of a person who'd grown up wealthy and powerful. The salt-and-pepper hair and wire-rimmed glasses underlined his classy appearance. His impeccable manners, the cultured voice, and the way he'd called out Tretter's faux pas solidified Anna's high opinion of him. It was obvious that he was not only a skilled scientist, but also schooled in the finer arts.

A few more persons joined them and soon the conversation turned to the Nazi ideology of the Master Race. Doctor Tretter made it a point to agree with and repeat whatever Professor Scherer or other high-ranking Nazi officials said. Anna couldn't hide a smile when she noticed that the professor wasn't overly impressed by T the devil's blatant efforts to win him over. In fact, he politely suffered the doctor's dialog.

Anna would have been able to join in the conversation, since genetics was one of her favorite topics, but she chose to remain quiet and listen in. And with every minute that passed, her admiration for Professor Scherer grew. In contrast to most of the others present he didn't appear to be a fanatic follower of the Nazi ideology, and often objected to any outrageous claim about the inferiority of certain races, with a hint at scientific research that hadn't been able to prove such claims. He worded his phrases carefully so as to not openly discredit any of the guests.

"We know accurately only when we know little; with knowledge doubt increases," the professor quoted.

Anna heard the words and turned to look at him with a raised brow. "Goethe?"

"Very good, my dear. You are familiar with his writings?" The professor smiled at her, obviously relieved to change the topic from ludicrous ideology to something more substantial.

"Some of them, yes." Anna felt a blush rising to her cheeks as the professor glanced at her with new interest.

"Oh, I love a good conversation about literature. Who is your favorite author?"

Anna didn't have to contemplate the question. "Schiller." Her younger brother Richard was the bookworm of the family and before he'd been sent to war, he tended to spend hours with his nose in a book. She smiled at the memory of how he enacted his favorite plays, assigning his three sisters minor roles as stage extras.

"Schiller, a comrade-in-arms of Hitler. Heil Hitler!" Hans Fabricius, head of section in the Ministry of the Interior, mentioned the book he'd written in 1932: *Schiller als Kampfgenosse Hitlers*.

Anna pictured Friedrich Schiller rotating in his grave. He'd never endorse his work being used to justify mass murder. A few of the men started a conversation about how both Schiller and Goethe would have supported National Socialism, had they lived one hundred and fifty years later.

Even though the conversation had steered away from him, Doctor Tretter wasn't finished with his lame attempts to butter up the professor. He took a step away from the rest of the group, before saying, "Your work in genetics is outstanding, Professor."

"It is based on Mendel's Laws. I daresay you have studied those?" the professor said. A glimmer in his eyes betrayed how much he loved to talk about his research.

"I have read everything about Mendel's work that I could get hold of," Anna couldn't help but say.

"Please forgive my inquiry, but aren't you working as a nurse?" The professor raised an eyebrow, apparently in disbelief at the idea that a nurse grasped an understanding of the complicated laws of genetics.

"I am, Professor, but more out of need to help the war effort than out of passion. My dream is to become a biologist one day." Anna smoothed her hands over her skirt to hide her nerves.

The professor gave her a scrutinizing glance. "And what area attracts your attention the most?"

"Human biology. Eradicating diseases with new treatments. And genetics, to gain a better understanding of hereditary diseases."

Doctor Tretter scoffed. "The solution to this is to prevent those tainted with bad blood from procreating. Then there's no need to *understand* exactly how damaged their offspring will be. The Master Race can only be achieved when we relentlessly pursue and annihilate the inferior elements."

Anna shuddered. Annihilating what the Nazis considered inferior elements was what the evil machine did day after day. The same machine she'd willingly become a part of to save her sister.

"Unfortunately, creating a pure and healthy race has suffered some setbacks. Eugenics might seem to be the answer, but as Mendel discovered, there are things the eye can't see that must be taken into consideration," Professor Scherer said and turned toward Anna. "Fräulein Klausen, let's see if you recognize this writer: *There is no such thing as chance; and what seems to us merest accident springs from the deepest source of destiny.*"

"Schiller," Anna answered.

"Right you are. Research has proven that there are diseases that can be avoided by careful breeding and isolating the affected individuals, but recessive genes often skip one or even several generations before rising again."

"But our Führer has taken care of this problem by creating the Aryan Master Race," Doctor Tretter insisted, and Anna half expected him to shout out another Heil Hitler.

"Yes, Doctor, our Führer has great visions, but so far we have only one generation to observe and we do not know what might become of the second or third generation," the professor answered.

"And if the diversity in the gene pool is too small, this might cause problems with new hereditary diseases in the future," Anna said.

"You seem well versed in the subject," the professor said, complimenting her.

"Thank you." Anna blushed at the compliment from the expert on genetics and felt as if she'd received a Christmas gift. She soaked it in, wanting to pinch herself to see if she'd been dreaming.

The camp commandant SS-Hauptsturmführer Fritz Suhren approached their small group. "Excuse me, Professor, but I must sequester Doctor Tretter for a few minutes."

The professor nodded and Anna almost jumped with excitement. From the look on the commandant's face it was clear that he wanted to speak with T the devil in private.

"You have a lovely home," she said to fill the ensuing silence.

"Thank you. It belonged to a well-known publisher, Louis Ullstein, before he emigrated." The professor adjusted his glasses with a sad look before continuing, "He used to host regular literary discussions. But his kind wasn't welcome here anymore."

"Not welcome? The Jews are responsible for the decline of the German culture. Our Führer will put a final solution to the Jewish problem once and for all." Doctor Tretter had returned far too soon, showering them with more Nazi ideology.

"Of course I agree with our Führer's point of view, but isn't complete annihilation a bit harsh?" Professor Scherer asked, apparently uncomfortable. Anna got the impression that this Louis Ullstein had been more than a random acquaintance to the professor.

"We can't make exceptions. Every last Jew has to be forced

from this earth or he will come back to haunt and destroy us." Anna tuned out Tretter's continued spoutings of Nazi ideology. What did he mean with a final solution? Complete annihilation? It couldn't mean...no. It was a ridiculous idea. Killing not thousands but millions of people just wasn't feasible.

It wasn't. Or was it?

CHAPTER 5

"F räulein Klausen, have you met everyone?" The professor waved an arm to encompass the members of their small group.

"No, I'm sorry, I have not." Anna shook her head.

The professor clucked his tongue and immediately set about introducing her to several high-ranking Nazi officials and their wives, and everyone was nice to her. As the evening wore on, her earlier worries about being under-dressed – which she clearly was – faded into the background and she enjoyed mingling among the guests. The luxurious attire and sparkling beauty of the guests in attendance were such a welcome respite from the walking dead she had to deal with on a daily basis.

She bit into a delicious hors d'oeuvre and wondered when she'd last seen such an abundance of food. For some people, rationing didn't seem to exist. She overheard the wife of a general complain about the recent lack of oranges. *Recent? I haven't seen an orange in years.*

Several times throughout the evening she had the chance to converse with Professor Scherer, and he was clearly flattered by her interest in and understanding of his research.

Late in the evening another guest made his appearance. Anna found her eyes continually drawn to him and wondered why nobody else took notice. Despite his nondescript black suit his presence filled the room, and a readiness lurked in his eyes that said he meant trouble with a capital T.

The man had the build of a wrestler: tall, broad shoulders, strong neck, and hands at least double the size of hers. His dirty blond hair was cut into a military short style, giving him a dangerous look emphasized by his dark beard and mustache. When he caught her staring into his glacial blue eyes, heat broke out in her body. His glance transfixed her and she had the disconcerting thought that he saw right through her carefully administered façade.

"Wolf!" The professor's voice pulled the man to attention.

"Yes, sir?"

"Have you seen that the automobile is ready?" the professor asked and the man nodded.

"Who is that?" Anna asked one of the women standing beside her eating canapés at a high table.

"Who?" the woman, clad in a royal blue evening gown and a sparkling diamond necklace, asked.

"The man talking to Professor Scherer."

"Ahh…that's Peter Wolf, his right-hand man. He acts as driver, assistant, and security guard."

Anna nodded, wishing to come up with something else to ask, but her mind drew a blank. The women didn't skip a beat, and continued their previous conversation as if the man truly didn't exist. *Doesn't anyone see how dangerous he is?*

Peter Wolf lingered at the professor's side, seemingly not taking part in the conversation. But every time Anna hazarded a glance his way, she noticed him listening intently. Studying. The few times their glances met, she felt like a lightning bolt seared through her. This Peter Wolf was indeed a disconcerting man.

Doctor Tretter sent her a dark stare from across the room and she hurried to his side, hiding a yawn.

"Fräulein Klausen, you look tired. Let me have my driver bring you home," the professor offered.

A rush of excitement coursed through her veins, but Anna knew better than to take him up on his offer. She shook her head saying, "That is very kind of you Professor Scherer, but Doctor Tretter will deliver me back home in due time."

"I was about to suggest to Nurse Anna that we should bid our goodbyes, since she needs to be at her work before dawn," T the devil said with a hidden glint in his eyes. Anna's stomach flipped over in fear. "Professor, thank you for a lovely evening."

"It's been my pleasure. We will be in touch about your conclusion in the gangrene research." Then Professor Scherer turned to Anna and kissed the back of her hand once again. "It was a pleasure meeting you, Fräulein Klausen. I could use someone like you on my scientific team."

"Don't you have enough nurses at university clinic to care for the health of you and your team?" someone asked, and the entire group laughed at the joke.

Anna didn't let the ridicule bother her and answered nonchalantly, "It would be an honor working for a renowned scientist like you, Professor."

On the drive back, a tense silence crackled inside the car. Doctor Tretter cursed a few times as the automobile skidded on the dark and icy road. The dim reflections of the moon and stars in the snow provided the only source of light. Wafting wisps of mist doused the landscape with eerie shadows.

While T the devil focused on the road, Anna clung to Professor Scherer's words to fill her soul with hope for a better future. It didn't matter whether he'd merely been polite or had really meant it. His compliments shone a ray of light on her otherwise dark existence.

Doctor Tretter drove past the nurse's dormitory and parked in front of his building. From the outside, both buildings looked the same, but of course the living quarters of the ranking officials consisted of more than a single room with a shared bath.

Anna sighed, every muscle tensing with dread.

He would rape her tonight again.

For a few hours she had forgotten about this perpetual nightmare, and even deluded herself that she could get away from all of this. But now, she followed him into his living quarters, hung her greatcoat on the coatrack, and put her purse, gloves, and hat on the table in the living room. Hugging herself to keep her arms from shaking, she stood there waiting for his orders. Doctor Tretter strode into the kitchen and poured himself a glass of wine, before he returned to look at her.

"You've been good tonight, Anna. The professor was

quite smitten with you, and this will surely help me in my quest to receive the professorship at the Charité. So now it's my turn to be *good* to you." His greedy leer made her toenails curl. Anna didn't know what was worse, when he showered her with all his sadistic cruelty, or when he was intent on making her *enjoy* the abuse. "Now get undressed, and wait for me in bed while I finish my wine."

Anna nodded and crossed the sitting room. She hesitated a split second, but the feeling of T the devil's stare boring into her back made her cross the threshold to the room where she'd endured the most awful ordeals.

Tonight would be no different.

Anna's soul left her body, and she returned to the soirée and the delightful conversations with Professor Scherer. *I could use someone like you.* She smiled and thought about all the possibilities and the hope the professor had planted in her heart and mind. Her mind engaged in a vivid dispute with him about the latest research into bacteria and possible anti-bacteria, and she burned with pride as he praised her for her good work.

"That was good, wasn't it?" Doctor Tretter's voice and a painful pinch into the delicate skin of her breast interrupted the dream. She didn't remember him coming into the bedroom, and she certainly didn't remember what he'd done to her body. She nodded to avoid further correction.

"Now get dressed and get out of here." He rolled to his side and started snoring within moments.

Anna stirred herself back to the present and pushed herself up on the bed, holding back the moan of pain that threatened to escape her mouth. *The man is a monster, and yet I let him rape me day after day.* For a fleeting moment, she considered stabbing a knife into his carotid artery, but she couldn't do it. She wasn't a cold-blooded murderer.

Several minutes later she slipped out of his apartment and hurried to her own room on the other side of the yard. This late at night, the entire camp was silent. Silent enough for one to ignore its mere existence. To pretend that the living nightmare wasn't real. That thousands of prisoners didn't suffer every day. That the annihilation of entire groups of the population was just a morbid notion.

But it *was* real.

And she knew it. And in the morning she had to face it all over again. She wasn't the driving force of the machinery, but she still played her part as cog in the wheel, and that weighed on her conscience.

Anna wept tears of regret, wishing she could flush out the guilt that lingered over what she'd become. She eyed the phone and considered calling Ursula to share the brighter events of the evening with her. But it was way past midnight, and if Ursula wasn't working, she would be fast asleep.

No, it was better to kindle the flame of hope within her heart, and not risk having it ripped apart by sharing it with another person.

CHAPTER 6

The next morning, Anna woke with a smile on her lips. Her inner light was still shining bright when she left for work. Her good mood was so obvious, even her fellow nurses teased her about a new man in her life. It was true, just not in the way they imagined.

Anna participated in the morning roll call, counted the sick women and the dead, and then went about her daily duties in the hospital ward. The roll calls should have been less time-consuming, because so many prisoners died every day. But it seemed for every dead woman, two new ones arrived in the cattle train transports.

Her heart always constricted when she saw the agonized faces of the newcomers. As if none of them had ever imagined earth could be worse than hell. Anna quickly learned to distinguish those who arrived from other concentration camps from those who were seeing the inside of a camp for the first time. It wasn't only the haggard and gaunt appearance of the veterans, but also the extinguished light behind their eyes. It was if they had long ago left this world, and only their pathetic physical shell remained.

And there was nothing Anna could do.

As the day wore on, more and more women wandered into the prison hospital, too sick or weak to work. Anna had never wanted to become a nurse, but she'd always wanted to help and heal. Her powerlessness to do so burned in her chest like a hot coal.

When lunchtime arrived, she walked with the other nurses to the canteen, where prisoners served the food. Anna never looked at them. Making eye contact would force her to acknowledge the hunger in their eyes. It must feel like abject cruelty to serve food to others while voracious hunger gnawed at your intestines.

Some of the prison's employees, though, took great pleasure in further augmenting the prisoners' misery. At the next table, a particularly sadistic guard offered one of the prisoners a bite of food, and then whipped her when she stretched out her hand to take it. Anna's stomach churned and she got up from her seat, pushing her half empty tray into the hands of one of the prisoners, hoping she would find a way to shove the food into her mouth without being seen.

In dire need of breathing fresh air that didn't smell of death and disease, she left the camp through the front gate, as another trainload of women arrived. *To hell with Hitler!* Anna cursed silently. She hoped there would be a special place for him somewhere that was a million times worse than Ravensbrück.

The remaining fifteen minutes of her lunch break didn't leave her many options, so Anna turned to the left, where a small artificial lake bordered by poplars lay calm and peaceful. The lake had frozen in the icy January temperatures and children from the nearby town of Ravensbrück skidded along the ice, playing tag. Alas, the refreshing sight of normalcy couldn't last.

As she returned to the barracks for the sickbay a guard rushed inside, breathing heavily.

"Is there an emergency?" one of the nurses asked.

"No." The young woman shook her head. "The camp commandant wants to see Nurse Anna right away."

Anna's heart froze in her chest as she turned and looked at the guard. "Hauptsturmführer Suhren?"

"Yes, are you Nurse Anna?"

"I am." Anna nodded, avoiding the anxious looks being sent her way by her colleagues. "What is this about?"

"I don't know but you must come with me now."

Anna buttoned up her greatcoat again and followed the guard, wiping her sweaty palms on her coat. Each step felt like a thick mud coated the ground, holding her feet hostage. Her mind raced, thoughts tumbling over each other, trying to determine what she could have done wrong. Had someone snitched on her for leaving food on her plate before handing it to the kitchen prisoner? Had her smile this morning raised a suspicion? Or...had Doctor Tretter made good on his threat to have her executed?

As she entered the prison command center, trailing after the guard, she could barely stop her hands from trembling. Simply keeping her breathing even took all of her concentration. Nurses were never summoned to the camp commandant's office, unless they'd committed a major transgression. She'd never witnessed this, but the other nurses knew of two instances and both times the nurse summoned had later walked down the execution corridor.

"The commandant will see you now," the secretary said and pointed to the door besides her desk.

Anna clasped her hands, telling herself that no matter what happened next, she would be strong and face it with her head held high. She took one hesitant step and then another, letting her feet carry her into the room where her future was most likely already decided.

Her eyes trained on her feet, she entered the office where she'd been only once before. On the day she started working at the camp.

"Heil Hitler," a male voice, not unfriendly, said.

Anna repeated the greeting and raised her head in dread to look at the man. She almost jumped backwards when a smiling Professor Scherer stood next to the commandant.

"You wanted to see me?" she muttered, her eyes jumping from one man to the other and back.

"Yes, Fräulein Klausen, please sit." Hauptsturmführer Suhren walked over to a small table with three chairs and gestured for her to do the same. With her heart thumping hard against her rib cage, she took a seat.

"Professor Scherer has approached me with a rather exceptional request." Suhren scratched his chin as if he couldn't understand the conundrum that lay at his feet. "He has asked me to consent to your transfer, working at his research department at the Charité. Provided that you agree."

Anna's jaw fell to the floor. "Me? Of course I agree." She glanced at Suhren, who didn't seem too happy about the situation, and hastily added, "It's not that I dislike working here, Hauptsturmführer, but if my service can support the war effort better elsewhere, than I will be the last person to object." She cast her eyes downward in an effort not to jump to her feet and scream her joy.

"In fact, I have spoken to the minister of education and science, and he agreed with my need for a capable nurse like Fräulein Klausen for my research staff at the Charité," Professor Scherer said.

Anna vaguely remembered that she'd been introduced to Reichserziehungsminister Rust the previous night at the soirée. She smiled at both men at the table, thinking that Professor Scherer hadn't become the stellar scientist he was by biding his time and placing decisions in the hands of others.

The number of subordinates one commanded was a direct sign of power, and nobody liked to lose an employee, much less cede one to another person. But since the professor had secured assistance from higher authorities, the camp commandant had to grin and bear it.

"Well then, it is agreed," the professor said; "Fräulein Klausen will come to work with my staff starting this coming Monday."

Anna nodded, still stunned at the speed of the events. "It will be an honor to work for you. I have always admired your work." Then a chilling thought crossed her mind and her blood froze into icy clumps. *T the devil! He will not like this.*

As if Suhren had read her mind, he walked over to his

desk and picked up the phone. "Can you please send Doctor Tretter to see me now?"

It took less than five minutes before a knock on the door indicated the arrival of her tormentor. Despite knowing he wouldn't dare touch her with the two higher-ranking men in the same room, a tremble ran through her limbs.

The secretary announced Tretter's arrival and moments later he strode through the door in his black leather boots. He scowled when he saw her and his expression darkened when he spotted the professor. "I'm not sure what Nurse Anna has done but I can assure you it will be dealt with—"

"Fräulein Klausen has done nothing, Doctor Tretter. Calm yourself," the camp commandant said. "Professor Scherer has requested that she join his research team in Berlin. And since all of us want to support his war-relevant work, I am happy to help out."

Liar. You would scratch out his eyes if you weren't wetting your pants because the Reichserziehungsminister approved my transfer.

Doctor Tretter sent a stare that promised tremendous consequences Anna's way and then shook his head saying, "With all due respect, Hauptsturmführer Suhren, I need her here. We're already short-staffed as it is."

"You'll have to do without her. It's not like you're actually caring for your patients," Suhren said with a cruel smile. "Fräulein Klausen will be leaving her post with us and starting her new position in one week's time."

"As you wish." Doctor Tretter clenched his hands by his sides, but bowed his head in a sign of agreement.

Anna swallowed and then took a moment to speak to the professor. "Thank you, Professor Scherer, for your confidence. I will see you in a week's time and I promise, I won't let you down."

"I know you won't," the professor said, smiling his approval.

"There's work to do," Tretter reminded her from the door, which he held open.

Anna nodded and preceded him through the door. She walked at a fast pace hoping to postpone the coming confrontation until he'd calmed down, but as they passed by a vacant barracks, he caught up to her and shoved her roughly around the side of the building.

"I'll give it to you, you snake in the grass." His hand tightened around her throat and panic crawled up her spine.

"Please, this was a shock to me just as much as it was to you," she stammered.

"I don't believe you for a second," he said and loosened his grip for a moment. Anna took a deep breath, but was too frightened to put up a fight. He noticed the panic in her eyes and a cruel smile appeared on his lips as his expression changed from angry to aroused. Anna's panic intensified when he put one hand beneath her great coat. "I do like you like this."

"Is there a problem here?" A deep voice barked the question, and Anna had never been happier to see two SS guards aiming their rifles at her.

"No problem, I'm the head physician," Doctor Tretter said, turning around, straightening to his full height. "My nurse had a nervous breakdown, but I believe she is better now. Isn't that right, Nurse Anna?"

"Yes, everything's fine now." Anna nodded and ducked

around his arm to hurry back to the sickbay before he could stop her again.

"The nurses are sissies, why do we even need them here?" one of the guards said.

"I wouldn't allow my girl to work. A good woman has to stay at home, tending to her husband and her children," the other one answered.

The rest of the day passed in a blur. Anna had a hard time hiding her excitement. It seemed her stars had aligned, changing her destiny. She would hold onto this chance of a lifetime with both hands and prove to Professor Scherer that she was worthy of his support.

In the evening, she walked to her small room with a newfound bounce to her step, bursting with the need to share the serendipitous change in her life. But unfortunately the last heavy air raids on Berlin had taken a toll on communications and Mutter's phone line was dead. Worry etched itself into Anna's mind and she dialed with trembling hands the number of the prison where Ursula worked.

"Schneider, Prison Plötzensee," Frau Schneider, Ursula's superior answered.

"Anna Klausen, I'm the sister of Ursula Hermann. Please forgive me for calling, but the phone line at home is dead and I was worried if the last bombing…" Anna left the rest of the sentence unspoken.

"Your sister arrived well and alive at work, so no need to worry," the woman on the other end of the line answered.

"Please forgive me for calling, but–"

"We're all worried. Thankfully, nothing bad happened. Soon enough our Luftwaffe will send the Englishman packing. Good evening."

"Good evening, Frau Schneider, and thank you."

Reassured, Anna sat in her only chair to write a letter to Mutter and Ursula about her fantastic news. Much later, she fell asleep with a smile upon her face, her dreams full of the marvelous things she was going to accomplish in the years to come.

CHAPTER 7

I t was over! Anna had been counting the days, hours, and then minutes until she could leave this ghastly place for so long, she could hardly believe the time had finally arrived. She folded the last of her personal clothing items into her suitcase and shut the lid. The nurse's uniform would have to stay, but she didn't mind. The fewer reminders of her time here, the happier she would be.

T the devil had outdone himself throughout the past six days, thinking of new cruel ways to make her suffer. More than once she'd reached her limit, and only the knowledge that her martyrdom was about to end had kept her going.

Professor Scherer's car would arrive any minute to take her to Berlin, her new job, and her new life. The sound of a car horn pulled her from her daydreams about the magnificent experiences that lay ahead, and she hurried down to the street.

Anna gasped at the sight of a gorgeous black Mercedes limousine waiting out front – the same kind of automobile that could be seen in propaganda pictures, the ones the Führer himself and his ministers used. She'd never seen such a fine vehicle up close and had never imagined she might actually be a passenger in one.

A queasy feeling passed through her stomach, but she ignored it as admiration of the fine automobile shoved it aside. The shiny black paint, a black leather convertible top that was tightly closed due to the cold temperatures beckoned her to climb aboard. White-walled tires sparkled with brightness and the chrome grill guard on the front reflected the sun shining from a clear blue sky.

To Anna, it looked like heaven on wheels.

A big man dressed in a dark suit with brass buttons and a driver's cap stood waiting for her. She peeked inside at the tan leather seats, wondering where the professor was. As she took a step towards the automobile, the driver raised his head and her pulse sped up as she started into the glacial blue eyes of Peter Wolf.

He strode over, taking the suitcase from her clenched fingers and stowing it in the trunk of the automobile with panther-like movements. Then he opened the rear passenger door and gestured with a hand for her to get in.

"Herr Wolf...where is the professor?" she asked, her heart thumping like crazy.

"The professor left two days ago on a business trip. Are you ready to go, Fräulein Klausen?" he said with a gravelly voice that slithered down her spine. It was comforting and disturbing at the same time.

She'd never had such a visceral reaction to a man before, and while his physical appearance enticed her, she sensed something else lurking underneath the surface. He wore the same expression she often used to convince someone of her innocence while she lied through her teeth. This man owned dark secrets.

"I don't…I didn't know the professor wasn't coming," Anna stammered, as her composure spiraled into a full-blown panic. What if this rescue was a ruse? What if Herr Wolf had been sent to kill her…or worse? It was a two-hour drive to Berlin, through mostly uninhabited areas. He could stop at any moment and nobody would ever be the wiser.

"Come, we should leave. I won't bite," Herr Wolf said as if he'd read her thoughts.

Anna nodded and his lips curled into a smile. If it weren't for those intense blue eyes, she'd feel calmer. They were eyes she was sure had seen things nobody should have to witness. Eyes that concealed the truth. Eyes that made her squirm.

She took a deep breath and slid inside the automobile. Professor Scherer wouldn't put her into the custody of a serial killer, and this man wouldn't dare to harm his boss's new employee. At least that was what she hoped.

Herr Wolf took the driver's seat and started the motor. But despite the comfortable interior and monotone humming of the Mercedes, she couldn't relax. The man intrigued her.

"Are you happy to be returning to Berlin?" he asked after steering the automobile onto the main road.

Anna nodded and then realized he probably couldn't see her. "Yes. I'm happy to be leaving the camp."

"Working there was hard?" His gravelly voice contained a curious undertone.

"I…working around so much death without the ability

to do anything about it was hard." She realized after speaking that her words could be interpreted two different ways, but when he didn't appear alarmed or question her further, she relaxed a bit.

"The professor said you had a place to stay in Berlin? Can you give me the address?"

Anna jerked her head up. *Why does he want my address?* But then it occurred to her that he was ordered to deliver her to Berlin, and he couldn't very well drop her off in the middle of Kurfürstendamm with her suitcase. His boss surely wouldn't approve of that.

"I live with my mother and sister." She gave him her address and then added, "I'm sure they are expecting me."

He must have noticed her fear, because he said with a chuckle, "Professor Scherer asked me to deliver you safely to your place – if that's what has you worried?"

"How did you know?" Anna clasped a hand over her mouth, but the words already hung in the air between them.

"It's my job to know everything Fräulein Klausen. Or do you prefer Nurse Anna?" Anna couldn't see his face, but nonetheless she *heard* the amused smile in his voice. And sensed the delightful trembles it sent through her body.

"Just Anna would be fine," she answered, hoping he wouldn't find it inappropriate.

"Anna." He pronounced her name like a verbal caress, lingering over every letter. For a moment, she thought she noticed an accent in his voice, but that must have been her imagination. "That's a beautiful name. Please do call me Peter."

"Peter. Have you been working for the professor for long?" she asked, striking up a conversation.

"It depends what you consider long. You will enjoy working for him, I should think. Professor Scherer is a generous man and treats his employees well."

"I'm very grateful for the offer to work on his team. I've always dreamt about becoming a biologist one day," Anna said and waited. Usually at this point the other party would answer something along the lines of *A woman becoming a scientist?* and laugh. Like the guests at Professor Scherer's soirée had done.

"I'm sure you'll make your way," he said, and then, after a few minutes of silence, "Are you originally from Berlin?"

"Yes. I love this city...or I love what it was before the war." Anna beamed with pride and gushed about all the fantastic things the capital offered, or used to offer, before the Allied bombers had done their best to reduce it to rubble night after night. The one good thing about her stay in Ravensbrück had been that the town had been spared the shelling and ensuing destruction. But even from this far away, she'd witnessed the orange glowing night sky over her beloved city. Every time her heart had been squeezed with worry for her loved ones.

"What about you? Where are you from?" she asked.

Peter shrugged his shoulders saying, "I moved about quite a bit, but now I live in Berlin."

It struck Anna again that he was hiding something. She'd also noticed the tension creeping into his neck muscles, making it all too clear that she shouldn't ask further questions about his origin. Nowadays even being born on the wrong side of the tracks could cause problems.

Maybe he was a *Mischling*, someone with one or more Jewish grandparents. She scrutinized his profile to search for the typical traits of the Jewish race. But then she laughed at her own stupidity. She'd been immersed in Nazi ideology too long and forgotten her scientific knowledge. Not all Jews had big noses and dark hair. Not even half of the Jewish prisoners at Ravensbrück looked remotely like Jews. But then, after several weeks in the camp, they didn't even resemble humans anymore. Anna had barely recognized her own sister Lotte when she'd seen her for the first time in the camp. A sigh escaped her, as memories threatened to break through.

"Are you alright?" Peter asked and turned to look at her.

"Yes. No need to worry," she answered and rested her forearms on the back of the front seat. Peter moved his hand as if he wanted to touch her elbow, but then returned it to the steering wheel.

"You're wearing a gun!" Anna blurted out, after catching a glimpse of the pistol strapped beneath his arm.

"A Mauser. Yes. It's just in case," he answered.

"Just in case of what?" Anna clasped her hands together. She couldn't help it, but the sight of the smooth black weapon brought the sound of clicks and handguns firing to her mind. Click and shoot. A cry. The sound of a collapsing body. She put a hand across her eyes.

"I've never used it," he added, turning around. His glance was meant to reassure, but Anna didn't believe him for one moment. Deep inside his eyes she could see the truth. Maybe he had never used this particular weapon, but he had killed before. Fear trickled down her spine, and she leaned back in her seat, her mind running in circles as she tried to work out why the professor's driver would need to wear a gun.

"This is the street?" he asked some time later, as he entered the street where she lived.

"Yes. That tall building over there." Anna wasn't sure whether she could trust him or not. While he'd never done anything to deserve her suspicions, she just *knew* there was more to him than everyone else seemed to see.

He parked in front of the building and then opened his door and came around the automobile to open the door for her. Then he retrieved her suitcase from the boot.

"Which floor? I'll carry this up to the door for you," he offered with a smile.

Anna shook her head and grabbed the suitcase from his hands. She could already imagine the gossip should her nosy neighbor Frau Weber see a handsome man like Peter carrying her suitcase upstairs.

"I'd rather go alone. Thank you for the drive," she answered with a smile.

Peter gave her a small bow and tipped the brim of his hat towards her. "My pleasure. I hope to see you more often, Anna."

Anna nodded, a strange feeling taking hold of her. Then she hurried to the front door of the apartment building. The door swished shut behind her, and she paused for a moment. She was home again. It was time to forget the past and embrace the future.

CHAPTER 8

Anna had barely reached her floor when the door next to hers flew open and Frau Weber rushed out, all flailing arms and heaving bosom.

"Anna! I haven't seen you in ages. Are you back from your assignment to..." Frau Weber said in a voice like honey. So, neither Ursula nor Mutter had succumbed to her persistent attempts to find out where Anna had worked.

"Frau Weber, it's good to see you too. It looks like not much has changed here." *Certainly not your nosiness.* Anna turned to unlock the door to her own apartment, but Frau Weber wasn't finished with her inquisition yet.

"That was a very nice automobile. Who does it belong to? And who was that man?"

"Good afternoon, Frau Weber."

"Anna, your mother and sister didn't say anything about you coming home. Vehicles like that don't come around this neighborhood..."

"Frau Weber, I would love to answer your questions, but

I'm not at liberty to divulge any information. You know... highest orders," Anna whispered and had great difficulty in keeping a straight face at the sight of Frau Weber's jaw dropping to the floor. Her revelations left the rather portly woman at a loss for words, something Anna had never experienced before. "Have a good day."

Anna unlocked her door and fled from the stunned woman outside. Anna didn't care if Frau Weber thought she was involved with the Führer himself, as long as it kept her from her incessant harping.

She stepped into the small hallway, set her suitcase down, and then jumped a foot when Mutter and Ursula screamed in one voice, "Goodness, Anna! What's happened? Why are you here?"

"Didn't you get my letter?" Anna asked, slightly breathless, because Ursula grabbed her in a fierce hug, threatening to crush her ribs.

"No. We haven't received any mail for at least a week," Mutter said and embraced Anna in a much more reserved hug. "But I'm glad you're home."

"Me too." Anna said and took off her coat.

Her mother disappeared into the kitchen, to prepare a meal for the three of them. Once it was ready, they sat down around the kitchen table. This was the moment Anna had not been looking forward to, as she still hadn't figured out what to tell her mother. Still, it felt good to have people fussing over her and checking to see that she was in one piece.

Maybe her body, but not her soul.

"Your sister has refused," Mutter said, sending a dark

stare towards Ursula, "to tell me what exactly you were doing in Ravensbrück."

"Nurse at the prison hospital; basically the same job I did here in Moabit." Anna forked half a potato into her mouth, hoping to gain time. Her ears burnt violently at the lie, but thankfully her mother wouldn't be able to see them beneath her long blonde hair.

"Anna!" Mutter's scowl clearly indicated that she didn't need to observe Anna's ears to know the truth – that she was lying by omission.

"How long will you be visiting?" Ursula came to her rescue.

"Not visiting, I'm here for good." Anna beamed at them. "I've been transferred to the Charité."

"The Charité? Your father would be so proud of you." Mutter had tears pooling in her eyes at the mention of her prisoner-of-war husband.

Ursula sent Anna a calculated glance, but kept her mouth shut. After they'd finished eating and washed the dishes, Mutter left to run errands.

"Spill it!" Ursula asked as soon as they were alone.

"I'm okay. I'm home now." Anna took a calming breath. "I don't want to talk about that time in my life. Ever."

Ursula squeezed her arm and for a moment a whole world of sorrow passed through her eyes, but then she smiled again. "Then tell me about this sudden transfer."

"Nothing much to tell," Anna hedged. "I'm happy to be closer to home."

"As you should be. Does this have anything to do with the famous Professor Scherer, head of the research department at the Charité?"

So Ursula has done her research. Anna raised a brow, but then her excitement won over and she deluged her sister with a torrent of words, recounting every little detail – omitting T the devil's role – of the events since she'd first set foot into Professor Scherer's mansion. "Can you believe that he's giving me this incredible chance? Little me, Nurse Anna, working with his research staff at the prestigious Charité? Oh, Ursula, I promise I will work harder than I've ever done before in my life and prove to the professor that I'm worthy of his support. I might even be able to study at the university and receive a veritable degree...Imagine me gaining a doctorate or even a Nobel Prize!"

"Anna, don't you think it's a bit too early for that?" Ursula asked, but Anna only stared at her.

"You can never dream big enough. And I will prove to the world that a woman can do anything she wants if she puts her mind to it."

"You know I'll support you all the way, right?"

"Of course I do. And that's why I love you so much, *Schwesterherz.*" Pronouncing the words sister and heart reminded Anna of her other sister. "Have you heard from Lotte?"

"Alexandra wrote a letter that she arrived safely at the convent and is recuperating. It seems she's gaining weight and her health is improving."

"Thank God! It was high time to get her out of there." Anna sighed.

"Yes, it was." Ursula looked tired.

Something is troubling her. She would ask her sister, but not today. Today was about being happy to be back home. Whatever bothered Ursula could wait until tomorrow.

"Let's go out to a bar and get a drink," she said to her sister.

"A drink? With Mutter around? Let me make some tea instead and then we can unpack your things." Ursula turned and walked into the kitchen.

CHAPTER 9

Anna arrived early at the Charité, and like every day in the past weeks she paused a moment to admire the red brick building and to marvel at what a privilege it was to be able to work with Professor Scherer's team.

The modern building hadn't sustained any severe damage during the recent air raids. Anna knocked on wood at the thought and strode past the Pediatric Clinic, a building erected at the beginning of the century. Back then the architecture had been of novel design, and the huge successes the Charité enjoyed in the fields of bacteriology and hygiene were partly attributed to that design.

A towering lecture hall dominated the center of the complex; the wards for patients extended to one side, whereas the actual Polyclinic building occupied the other side of the huge campus. Another breakthrough novelty had been the separate row of quarantine barracks that were connected with a gangway to the normal wards. That gangway could only be passed by persons with special clearance and only under strict hygienic precautions.

In contrast to the rest of the complex, the quarantine barracks looked rather rundown from the outside, as no non-medical personnel were allowed to access the restricted area, in order to prevent the possible spread of diseases and outbreak of an epidemic.

Anna had never been in the quarantine barracks, and except for a short visit on her first day, she hadn't spent time in the patient wards either. The bacteriology labs were located in the part of the compound with restricted access to the public.

She approached the building and showed her employee card at the gate.

"Good morning." She greeted the doorman with a smile.

"You are early again, Fräulein Klausen," he answered and waved her past.

Since working here, she'd never had problems getting up in the morning. In fact, she jumped out of bed before the alarm went off, eager to start her day's work.

Greeting her coworkers, she changed into her lab coat and started to work. Since she'd been assigned to carry out different experiments with bacteria cultures, her first task in the morning was to examine what had happened during the night, write down her observations, and present conclusions.

Her conclusions would be revised by her supervisor, and every other day, Professor Scherer himself would check up on her progress. She had become used to the professor's encouraging words and the help he offered to all of his employees, but in the secret recesses of her heart, she yearned to see Peter.

"Anna, Professor Scherer wants to talk to you about the last experiment you completed," Peter said, sauntering into the lab and flashing her a huge smile.

Anna felt as if she'd conjured him up from the depths of her fantasies. Her heart always thumped in staccato when he burst in like this, partly from her attraction to him and partly from what still lay undiscovered underneath his twinkling eyes. But after a few days of working at the Charité she'd decided that a man working this closely with her admired mentor couldn't be a bad person.

"Good morning, Peter." She washed her hands with special soap and wiped them dry, before she walked over to where he stood. While it wasn't necessary or even usual to shake hands every day, she enjoyed the touch of his warm, calloused palm on hers too much to let the opportunity slip by her.

He seemed to feel the same way, because their handshake always lasted seconds longer than was appropriate. Today, he moved his thumb in a caressing gesture across the back of her hand, and she felt tingles spreading across her skin.

"You look beautiful today," he said with another of his devastating smiles.

Anna scoffed, but inside her heart sang. "You're a charmer." She knew very well that she didn't look her best in the white lab coat that made her pale skin look pasty, and wearing the white cap to contain her hair.

"How can you say that? You're the most beautiful

woman on earth," he said, putting his left hand across his chest with a mock expression of hurt.

Blood shot to her face. Well, at least she wasn't pale as a ghost anymore.

"I'd better not let the professor wait," she said, and pulled her hand out of his grasp. Then she rushed past him, butterflies wreaking havoc in her stomach. Minutes later she knocked on Professor Scherer's door, still slightly out of breath.

"Come in," his distinguished voice called out.

"You wanted to see me, Professor?" Anna entered the office that looked so different from all the other rooms in the Charité. Most of the doctors and professors who worked here had used the standard furniture. Not him. An immense mahogany desk occupied almost half of the space, with scientific magazines, research papers, and books stacked in neat piles on either side of the black writing mat. A glass of ink and an expensive-looking fountain pen lay at the ready to document his next brilliant thought.

"Yes, Fräulein Klausen. I've compared the results of your last week's experiments with the tuberculosis bacteria to a similar approach I've read here," he said, holding up a prestigious medical magazine, "and I think you're on to something."

"Oh," Anna muttered for lack of a better word.

"In fact, I think you should do another series of tests with a slightly different approach."

Anna took out a notebook and pencil and jotted down his suggestions.

"Come back to me as soon as you gather results. I believe

with the knowledge we'll learn from these iterations, we might see a breakthrough in treating this disease."

"Thank you, Professor." Anna beamed with pride.

"Don't thank me, Fräulein Klausen. You have done the brunt of the work. I merely hinted at the right direction to you." Professor Scherer stood to walk her to the door and added, "I'm glad to have you on the team."

She returned to the laboratory with a bounce in her step, intent on doing her share to find a cure for the dreadful disease of tuberculosis.

CHAPTER 10

In the next staff meeting, Professor Scherer announced that he needed to leave on a business trip and wouldn't be available for the next few days. Anna didn't mind not having the professor around, but she would miss Peter's regular visits, since the professor rarely left town without his trusted driver and personal security guard.

Much to her surprise, Peter later stopped by her lab with his usual grin.

"Peter, I thought you were gone with the professor?" she said, her heart taking a leap.

Not that I mind.

"We aren't leaving until early morning. And I couldn't leave without saying goodbye to you, now could I?" he asked and sauntered towards her.

The butterflies in her stomach did double dips as she noticed something purple in his hand, half hidden behind his back.

"You look peachy in that dress, Anna."

She glanced down at what he could see of her dress, hidden by the white lab coat she wore, and shook her head saying, "You can't see my dress as it's mostly covered up."

"Oh, well, maybe I meant to say you were peachy; therefore, anything you wear is by association peachy." He hovered dangerously near, and his presence made her all light-headed and silly.

Anna blushed and giggled. "What if I was wearing a burlap sack?"

"You would still be beautiful." He took yet another step and held out a single purple crocus for her. "I'm sorry, but that was all I could get."

"It's beautiful, thank you so much." Anna took the flower and turned away to hide her burning cheeks. She busied herself looking for a vessel to use as vase. When she found a test tube and filled it with water, Peter stepped beside her and covered her trembling hand with his.

"Would you go out with me tonight?" he said leaning in to her, his low voice sending sweet shivers up her spine.

"Go out with you?" Anna looked at him and blinked a few times, dumbfounded.

"Yes. On a date." He grinned at her, his eyes twinkling. "I want to spend time with you away from work."

Anna swooned, her knees wobbling so much she gripped the counter to steady herself. She should like his attention… she did like it…but at the same time, the memories she'd locked deep down in her soul threatened to bubble up every time she considered…

"People do that? They actually do other things besides work?" Anna asked with a raised brow.

"If you have to ask, then you definitely need to say yes,"

he insisted, taking the test tube from her and then holding both of her hands between his own strong palms, rubbing them with his rough thumb. Anna's heartbeat accelerated under the soft caress. "Please. I know you want to, I can see it in your eyes. Say yes."

"Yes," Anna's instinct answered before her rational brain had a chance to kick in and deny his request.

"Wonderful. I'll pick you up after work here. Or do you need to go home first?"

"Afraid I'll get away?" Anna teased him.

"Absolutely."

"Don't worry. I always keep my promises."

"That's my girl. See you soon." He let her hands go and then whistled his way out of the laboratory.

She watched him disappear from view and then did a little twirl behind her counter. Until the fierce grip of self-doubt and dark demons attacked her, choking away her joy. A few hours later, having made a trip to the ladies' bathroom to freshen up her face and hair, she returned to the lab to find Peter waiting for her.

"Ready to go?" He offered her his arm and led her outside. "So, what do you like to do for fun?" When Anna gave him an incredulous look, he revised his question, asking, "Hmm, let's rephrase this. If we didn't live in a city reduced to rubble with the worst war from time immemorial raging, what would you do for fun?"

Anna giggled. Peter had the refreshing ability to make her feel light, almost as if floating. Under the strength of his ministrations, darkness seemed to fade away. "Well, I like going to the motion pictures, and I like to dance. It's been such a long time since I did either one of those."

"There are still motion pictures to go see." They had already left the grounds of the Charité, and Peter wrapped his arm around her shoulders as they walked along the river Spree and towards the Reichstagsgebäude. The formerly magnificent building had never been fully restored after the mysterious fire in 1933, and the damage from the constant air raids had turned it into a shameful ruin, reminding the citizens of Berlin of the war raging across Europe.

"Propaganda films..." Anna said and stopped to look at him. She needed to know where he stood and how far she could go in voicing her repudiation of the things the government did. He held her glance and then nodded.

"I agree. But the war won't last forever."

"You sound so certain of that."

"I am. Everyone is. Let's get a bite to eat." He turned to continue walking along the Spree River to the bridge across and Anna pondered his answers. She couldn't put her finger on it, but something about his demeanor hinted that he did not approve of the Nazis. Not enough, though, to trust him with her own opinions.

Peter stopped in the middle of the heavily damaged bridge and looked down into the black water flowing lazily beneath them. Just weeks ago the river had still been frozen over, much to the delight of the children. They walked straight ahead until they reached the street to see and be seen on: Unter den Linden.

To the left lay the heavily damaged Brandenburger Tor, the Quadriga miraculously still on top of it, and to the right the formerly beautiful grand boulevard. Peter steered her towards a restaurant that had managed to remain unscathed amongst the rubble. While eating, Peter entertained her with small anecdotes about his work with the professor, and Anna told him how much she loved to work with Professor Scherer.

Peter listened with interest, but didn't talk much about himself, unlike most other men Anna knew, who could go on and on boasting about their importance. It endeared him even more to her, but a little doubt remained. Why did he avoid talking about his family or his upbringing? Maybe, she figured, his parents had died, and he avoided the resurfacing of painful memories?

"Thank you for such a lovely evening," Anna said as it was getting late. They still didn't have phone service at home and Mutter would worry if Anna returned too late.

"I'll see you home, before it gets dark," Peter said and paid for their meal, before he helped her into her coat and then offered his arm again.

She liked walking beside him, feeling his reassuring presence and the sparks coursing through her body. A kiosk stood behind the bus stop, radio blaring with the usual evening news. Despite the clear sky, the detested bomber pilots seemed to have taken a day off, because no air raid pre-warning was given. Anna shuddered and turned up her coat's collar.

The most important news of the day was the assassination of the SS and Police Leader of Warsaw, Franz Kutschera, by members of the Home Army, the Polish resistance moment. In reprisal, three hundred Polish civilians had been taken hostage in an attempt to expose the murderers. Even as the reporter spoke about the despicable crime committed against Kutschera and Germany, Anna felt Peter tense and almost crush her hand in his forceful grip.

"Peter? Are you alright?" The sight of his tightly set jaw and dark scowling eyes frightened her.

"I'm sorry." He glanced down at her hand and released it. "I hope I didn't hurt you."

"Just a bit, but are you sure you are fine?"

"I am. I should get you home now," he said and relaxed his facial muscles to send her a reassuring grin. A *fake* grin.

Anna couldn't fathom why the news of a random SS officer being assassinated in Warsaw had sent him off-kilter. It wasn't like these kinds of things didn't happen every day. How could a man who wore a loaded Mauser at all times be squeamish about a single murder? Unless...the victim had meant something to him.

Anna swallowed hard as fear settled deep into her bones. Had he been sent to spy on her?

CHAPTER 11

At home Ursula and Mutter were already waiting for her, with huge smiles on their faces that brushed away her own anxiety.

"Anna! Guess what happened!" Ursula said, bouncing up and down. Mutter waved a letter in her hand, answering her daughter's question before Anna could say a word. "A letter from Richard!"

"Richard?" Anna put a hand across her heart. Her younger brother, who'd been missing somewhere in White Russia since last fall, had sent a letter. "Let me see!" she demanded and took the paper with trembling hands from her mother. "It's dated Christmas 1943, that's almost two months ago." The words swam before her eyes and she couldn't decipher more than the greeting *Liebe Mutter.* She flopped onto the couch in the sitting room and her mother and sister both talked at once.

"His battalion was defeated near Minsk and most of his comrades died, but he and another one managed to get onto a train to Warsaw…" *Warsaw?* Anna thought, *that's where the SS leader was assassinated by partisans.* "…he's not in a combat unit currently…can't tell us where he is now…top secret… we can write letters to the German command in Warsaw… he's confident the war will soon be over." Anna tried to follow the conversation as Ursula and Mutter interrupted each other's sentences. But one thing was clear: her brother Richard was still alive.

She hugged them both and all three women shed tears of happiness. Knowing Richard's whereabouts took a huge burden from their shoulders.

When Mutter had taken to her room to write a letter to her only son, Anna found a frowning Ursula staring at her. "Where were you? You should have been home hours ago."

For a split-second Anna considered lying, but Ursula would undoubtedly see through her. "On a date."

"A date?" Ursula stumbled and had to grab onto the wall to steady herself. Being this clumsy was strange for Anna's usually ultra-perfect sister.

"Yes, a date. And before you ask, his name is Peter and he works for Professor Scherer," Anna added.

"Please be careful," Ursula urged her.

"Don't worry, he's nothing like…" An icy chill ran down Anna's spine, remembering the way Peter had almost crushed her hand earlier.

"I didn't mean…" Ursula cast her eyes downward before saying, "but he's a Nazi."

"You've never met him! How do you know he's a Nazi?" Anna glared at her sister, who wasn't the slightest bit intimidated. In their adolescent years they used to yell at each other all the time.

"Only high-ranking Nazis have automobiles these days, much less a Mercedes limousine."

"Just because Professor Scherer associates with the Nazis doesn't mean he's one himself. In fact, he does not support many of their ideas..." Anna shook her head. They'd already had this discussion several times. "And what does this have to do with Peter? He's only the driver."

"The driver for a Nazi. I see. That makes him automatically part of the resistance." Every single word from Ursula's mouth dripped with sarcasm.

"Please, Ursula, Peter is a good man," Anna pleaded.

"The jury's still out on that. What if he turns on you and you suffer the same fate as Lotte?"

Anna's temper flared. "Don't. Don't speak to me about Lotte. I gave up *everything* to save her. Me! I gave up everything..." She stopped talking as tears threatened to overwhelm her. "Including my self-respect. Please, I don't need you to tell me who I can and cannot see. I was hoping you might be happy for me."

"Anna, you don't know what you're saying. You need to stop seeing him. Think of what's at risk."

"I know better than you what's at risk. I lived it," Anna said.

Ursula didn't answer. She rushed into their room and when Anna followed her several minutes later, she could still hear her sobbing under the blanket. Ursula had been exceptionally grumpy and irritable lately, but Anna was too angry and tired right now to try and figure out the reason for her sister's drastic mood swings and continuous fatigue. The war was taking a toll on everyone.

She put on her nightgown and disappeared under her

own blanket, blocking out the sounds of Ursula's miserable sobs.

～

One week later Anna dashed home to tell Ursula exciting news. "Sister, guess what?"

"More good news?" Ursula lounged on the couch, her feet up and holding her back in pain as she turned around to Anna.

"I've been invited to attend the official celebration of freshly graduated military doctors at the Charité," Anna said and smiled at the thought that Peter, with whom she'd been walking out almost every day, would be there too and might even dance with her.

"Military doctors?" Ursula bit her lip. "It's an honor, but…you shouldn't go."

"Why on earth wouldn't I want to go to one of the few social dance events that are still held in Berlin?" Anna stared at her sister in disbelief.

"There will be all sorts of high-ranking Nazi officials there." Ursula sighed, making a face as if Anna couldn't understand a simple concept.

"I know, but it wouldn't be the first time I've socialized with them, and it probably won't be the last. You know, we live in the same country." Anna straightened her skirt and challenged her sister to object.

Ursula looked horrified, saying, "How can you say that? Since when do you like the Nazis?"

"I don't like them, but that doesn't mean I have to avoid

64

them at all costs. Apart from being something fun to look forward to, this event is important for my career."

"Your career? Is your career more important than your moral values?" Ursula rose to her full height, and planted her fists on her hips. In that position she looked different than normal, somehow bigger.

"Ursula, don't be ridiculous. It's just a celebration. Nothing to test my moral values." *Except maybe if Peter makes a move and kisses me.* Anna's cheeks stained themselves with heat and she hastily added, "I'm not becoming one of them, just because I attend a party."

"You could have fooled me," Ursula said sullenly, but the next moment she smiled. "Knowing how stubborn you are once you've set your mind on something, I guess I'd better save my breath."

"Thanks," Anna said, hugging her sister. "I hate fighting with you."

"Come with me," Ursula said, and gestured for Anna to follow her to their room. Once inside she opened her closet and took out her wedding dress, a dark blue woolen A-line skirt that ended mid-calf and a fitted jacket in the same color. "You'll need something nice to wear," she explained and handed it to Anna.

"That's such a moving gesture, darling, but I already have a dress," Anna said and reached into the bag she'd brought home with her to pull out a royal blue lace dress, holding it up in front of her. "What do you think?"

"Wow! It's precious! Where did you get that?" Ursula squeaked.

"Professor Scherer. He probably guessed I wouldn't have a

formal gown to wear, and offered to lend me one that belonged to his late wife." Anna didn't mention that Peter had been sent to the lab with three different dresses and his eyes had almost popped out of his head when she'd modeled them for him.

Ursula stepped forward and fingered the elegant material of the dress. "Italian lace," she whispered reverently as her fingertips slid across the intricate pattern. "This must have cost a fortune."

"I know. I tried to refuse the offer, but as soon as I tried it on at work, my resolve disappeared. It looks as awesome as it feels."

"So, you're going, no matter what I say?"

Anna sighed and nodded. "Yes. I'm going."

"Please be careful," Ursula said and hugged her tight.

CHAPTER 12

The day of the celebration arrived, and Professor Scherer had insisted Anna take half a day off to prepare herself for the formal evening. She'd arrived home and taken care with her makeup and hair, donning the dress a few minutes before Peter was due to pick her up in the professor's limousine.

"Good evening." Peter opened the passenger door for her and when he put his hand on her back to assist her getting into the vehicle, this time she didn't pull away. "You look absolutely gorgeous," he whispered into her ear before shutting the door.

"Thank you," she murmured when he got in the driver's seat. "You look very handsome tonight as well."

"I couldn't have you completely outshining me," he teased as he pulled back out into traffic.

Anna settled back in the seat with a smile. She'd grown to like Peter a bit more every day. He was so different from the slick, slimy men she worked with. Every one of her colleagues did his best to butter up his superiors, trying to meet some ideal he thought would gain him a higher position. And definitely none of them ever spoke out of line in their quest for a good standing and a fast promotion with the Nazi government.

But Peter was just … Peter. He was always true to himself – honest. Anna giggled at her own musings.

"What's so funny?" Peter asked with an amused glance.

"Actually, I thought how different you are from the men I work with." She turned to observe him and, right then, the artery in his neck started throbbing. It was one of the tell-tale signs that he was on alert. It appeared at the strangest moments, and Anna hadn't yet been able to figure out what triggered the raising of his guard.

But being the thorough researcher she was, she took another mental note. Eventually, she'd solve the entire puzzle that was Peter. *Being different, he wants to blend in.*

"Ahh, I would hope that I'm more dashing than your colleagues," he commented with a joking tone in his voice. But Anna knew him too well to be fooled. His carotid artery kept pulsating.

"Of course you are." She smiled and boldly put a hand on his arm. "But it's mostly your behavior. You behave differently." Anna had barely finished her sentence when she felt his entire body tense up. She decided to push further. "You're true to yourself."

Peter stopped the car in front of the Charité, and she could sense his growing discomfort and his need to stop the conversation. It was a pattern they'd gone through many times in the past weeks. But today she wasn't about to veer away. She increased the pressure on his arm, effectively

68

keeping him in place, squirming like a worm on a hook. "You never say something just because the other person wants to hear it. You're honest."

His eyes flickered. But he regained control almost instantaneously and smiled. "That's a pretty deep analysis of a simple driver. May I now escort the most beautiful woman on earth to the party?"

Like always, his smile did funny things to her, melting her resolve to unravel the mystery Peter Wolf presented. For now she was content to know that he lied – about what she wasn't sure – and nodded. "We wouldn't want to be late, now would we?"

Peter walked around the Mercedes to open the door for her, and extended his hand to help her to get out. Anna wasn't afraid of him anymore, but the more she got to know him the more she was convinced that he was a dangerous man.

"You're a knockout in that dress," he said, his eyes traveling up and down her body as he helped her out of her coat in the big foyer.

Anna blushed and looked up into his eyes. Right now they didn't hide anything. She took a step back to take in Peter's physique. His broad shoulders filled out the tuxedo jacket; the contrast between the crisp white buttoned-down shirt and the black suit with the satin lapels made him look all the more attractive. He fit in perfectly with everyone else, but Anna noticed the bulge under his jacket. The Mauser pistol. Peter was dangerous – deliciously dangerous where she was concerned.

Professor Scherer already waited for them in the large room decorated with swastikas and rods of Asclepius.

Uniformed waiters carried silver trays of champagne and offered one to Anna. As he seemed to always do, Peter faded into the background as soon as he reached Professor Scherer's side to serve as his security guard.

Anna had first been angry, then confused, and then stunned by the way people – even the waiters – seemed to see right through him as if he weren't even present.

"Fräulein Klausen, you look lovely in that dress," Professor Scherer complimented her. Since working for him she'd quickly become his favorite staff member, and he'd become a valuable mentor to her. Much to the dismay of her predominantly male colleagues, who thought the only acceptable place for a woman in the Charité was wearing a nurse's uniform and standing at a patient's bed.

"Thank you so much for making it possible for me to be here." Anna smiled, a hint of sadness sweeping over her. Professor Scherer had taken on a father role in her life, and on occasions like this she wondered whether she would ever see her own father again.

"Come, I will introduce you around," he said, taking her elbow and leading her further into the room. He made good on his promise, and Anna found her knees becoming like jelly when they came to stand in front of a group of highly decorated uniformed men, one of whom she recognized as Heinrich Himmler. The man who was responsible for facilitating and overseeing the concentration camps. Unsure whether or not it was expected of her to *Heil Hitler*, she waited until she was spoken to.

"Heinrich," Professor Scherer greeted the man as if he were a close friend, "may I introduce Fräulein Klausen to you. She is my newest scientific discovery, my star pupil, and I'm sure we will hear great things from her in the years to come. I found her at the camp in Ravensbrück, working for Doctor Tretter."

The mention of T the devil's name sent a physical punch to her stomach, but somehow Anna managed to stand upright and smile at the Reichsführer of the SS.

"Well, well, whoever said there's nothing good coming out of the camps clearly was wrong." Himmler held out his hand saying, "Very pleased to make your acquaintance, Fräulein."

Anna fought the urge to scratch out his eyes and glanced downward to hide her growing disgust. "It's my pleasure…" She had no idea about how to correctly address him and opted to use his position. "…Herr Reichsführer."

Thankfully Professor Scherer excused them and then went to introduce her to many more people, all of them apparently belonging to the inner Nazi circles, or at least to the wealthy people associating with the Party leaders.

In awe of all the power and wealth permeating the room, she searched for Peter, hoping a glimpse of him would ground her back in reality. Despite his external appearance's blending in perfectly, his presence stuck out like a sore thumb against the yea-sayers, blind followers, and enthusiastic Party members. But apart from Anna, apparently nobody even noticed him.

He sent her a grin, and she felt the confidence seeping back into her bones. She could fake her way into this elitist society. She hadn't honed her acting skills for nothing over the years. Anna made smart talk, returned the smiles people sent her, and slowly relaxed, until pride filled her chest when Professor Scherer introduced her again as his *star pupil*, despite the fact that she wasn't even technically one of his students. She hadn't been admitted to university – yet.

But I will. And when that happens...look out.

But the more she enjoyed herself, the louder a nagging voice in her head repeated Ursula's words. *They are Nazis. Stay away from them. You're either for them or against them. There's no in-between.* Anna brushed the pesky warnings away. Just because she enjoyed this celebration with all its splendor and razzle-dazzle didn't mean she liked the Nazis. She could very well differentiate, thank you very much.

As the evening wore on, she danced with several of the young medical graduates in their new and shining military uniforms, but the one man she longed to dance with was off limits. She glanced at Peter, who stood a few feet sideways to the professor, and almost giggled at the dark stare he sent her current dance partner. After this dance she excused herself, and walked over to a group of uniformed men in a heated discussion with Professor Scherer.

Anna only had eyes for Peter while she stood silently only half-listening to their conversation. When they mentioned that Admiral Canaris had been dismissed from his position as chief of the *Abwehr* several days earlier, she noticed how Peter's stance became rigid as he intently listened in on the speculations about the reasons and possible implications.

Himmler must know but he only mentioned that Canaris was currently in Burg Lauenstein, awaiting the bestowal of the German Cross in Silver and Hitler's new orders. The conversation soon turned to military topics and Anna couldn't believe her own ears.

Contrary to radio news of victories, the gathered military leaders talked about losses. Losses of lives, material, and land. Advances of the Eastern Front had been all but rolled back, the glorious German Wehrmacht outnumbered by the Red Army one to ten, overrun faster than they could retreat. Hundreds of thousands of German soldiers had been killed or captured.

A cold hand reached into Anna's heart. Her brother Richard was relatively safe in Warsaw, but for how long? If the Eastern Front had really crumpled like these generals indicated, the Russians would soon march into Warsaw and – God forbid – onto Germany's home soil.

Anna didn't like the Nazis, but the prospect of Red Army soldiers looting, raping, and murdering their way across her country frightened her even more. *No,* she thought and shook her head. Those men were exaggerating; it would never come to that. It *could* never come to that.

Her eyes sought out Peter's again, but this time his expression did nothing to reassure her. Hate waged a war in his striking blue gaze at the mention of violent combat in the East of Poland. Anna tuned out the talk of war and left the group again to find diversion in dancing with young and optimistic medical graduates. Their attitudes intrigued her, since all they wanted was to embrace life and enjoy the pleasures it offered to the fullest before being sent to the inevitable cruelty of the front.

CHAPTER 13

In the wee hours of the morning Professor Scherer escorted Anna to the waiting limousine and Peter's care. "Make sure she gets home safely."

"You know I will, Professor," Peter answered, assisting her into the back seat of the vehicle, before he asked the professor, "At what time shall I return for you?"

"Don't worry about me. I will see myself home. Fräulein Klausen, it was a pleasure having you here this evening. Goodnight." Professor Scherer performed a small bow and then returned inside.

Peter took the driver's seat and remained quiet until he had pulled out onto the streets. Due to blackout restrictions darkness enveloped the automobile, but still Anna could feel his eyes on her in the mirror.

She had no idea how he drove through the dark night with the dimmed headlights. Maybe his eyes adjusted to the poor lighting, and since there was hardly any traffic on the streets, including foot traffic, it probably seemed riskier than it actually was.

"Peter?" Anna whispered into the stillness of the night.

"Yes, Anna?"

"Could I sit up front with you?"

"Certainly." Peter chuckled and pulled over. A moment later he opened her door and pulled her from the vehicle and into his strong arms saying, "Are you spooked?"

"Not really, but it was rather lonely back here, with no lights on anywhere in the city..." She had no idea how to explain that she'd been missing the comfort of his nearness.

"You don't have to explain. I'd love to have you sit beside me." He opened the front passenger door and handed her back into the automobile before he hurried around to the driver's side.

After starting their forward movement once more, he reached across the seat and searched for her hand. Anna basked in the warmth emanating from him and when he tugged her over closer to him, she felt peace settle into her bones. "Thank you."

"For what? I didn't do anything."

It wasn't true. Being with him seemed to heal her weeping soul. By his side she could forget.

"Did you have fun tonight?" Peter asked after a while.

"A lot. I can't remember having had so much fun in years. It's not as if there are many chances to go out and dance these days."

"I wish I could have danced with you." He squeezed her hand and gave a slight chuckle, continuing, "Don't get me wrong, I want you to be happy, but I hated seeing you in the arms of all those young men. Young men that weren't me."

Anna giggled. "Don't tell me you were jealous."

"Not really... maybe a bit. Fine, I admit it. I'd rather have you all to myself." At his husky disclosure, Peter growled with such fierce possessiveness that her heart jumped and she wanted to yelp with joy.

He pulled up in front of her building and turned off the engine. When he made no move to get out, she gazed at him. His expression turned fiery, and he stared at her with desire flaming in his eyes. Her heart missed a beat or two. Images of another man kissing her flashed through her mind and she tensed.

No, I will not cloud this moment with regret and shame from the past.

The expression in Peter's eyes changed, became softer, as he reached up and fingered a lock of her hair that had escaped the pins of her elaborate hairdo.

"I want to kiss you," he said, his finger tracing its way down her cheek. A delicious tingle followed in the wake of his caress and suddenly the world stopped spinning. Time stood still as she waited with rapt anticipation to be kissed by him.

"Kiss me," she whispered and leaned into him. Moments later, his lips landed softly on hers and the overwhelming sweetness of his touch seeped deep into her soul. Anna struggled with the intensity of her emotions, and when he reached out to press her tighter against him, she instinctively jerked away.

"I should leave. It's late."

"What are you afraid of, sweetheart?" His voice was calm and soft, his hands holding hers in a reassuring grip.

I can't possibly tell him. Not when all I want is to forget. Cut my link to the past once and for all. She shook her head, a single tear rolling down her cheek.

"Anna, sweetheart. Don't cry, please." Peter used his finger to wipe the tear away. "I would never do anything to harm or scare you."

She nodded.

"Please promise to tell me if I ever do something that makes you feel uncomfortable. Will you?"

She nodded again.

"Good. Get some sleep and I will see you at work." Peter placed a kiss on the top of her head and asked, "Now should I walk you to your door?"

"Better not. I'd rather not give Frau Weber a reason for gossip." She cocked her head and pondered whether she should tell him about how her neighbor had called the Gestapo on the sisters, because she'd seen a man enter their apartment. *Maybe another time.* "Good night Peter. I did enjoy the kiss, it's just..." She sighed, at a loss for words. How did a woman explain to her new romantic interest that she'd been brutalized for so long, so tormented by a violent past, she didn't even remember what it was like to feel whole?

"No use sweating over it," Peter said.

Anna smiled, letting the moment pass, and then slipped from the Mercedes, quietly making her way into the building. Kissing Peter had been wonderful, but she needed time to process the emotions moving through her body. And sleep. She needed sleep.

~

The next morning, when Anna woke up late, Ursula was already waiting for her, tapping her toe on the floor in annoyance.

"How was the party?" She held out a mug with hot tea. "Sorry, not even *Ersatzkaffee* left in the house." Recently, even the ration cards couldn't buy anything anymore. Hundreds, maybe thousands of shops in the capital had closed, because their owners had been forced to leave or to work in war-related industries.

"It was wonderful and overwhelming all at the same time. There were so many important people there, and Professor Scherer introduced me to all of them."

Ursula grimaced and Anna could read her thoughts. *Nazis. All of them. You'd better stay away.*

"Not all of them are bad. I even met Reichsführer Himmler–"

"And what exactly is *not* bad about him?" Ursula's scathing comment cut through the air like a knife.

"Of course, he is evil. But there were others, recent graduate doctors–"

"–happily following Hitler into his monstrous war," Ursula completed her sentence.

It wouldn't make sense to tell her sister about the champagne, food like there was no shortage, exotic fruits most Germans had forgotten existed, and real chocolate.

"Professor Scherer has promised to promote me; he may even help me to get accepted into university. Can you imagine?" Anna beamed with pride, but her sister's face went from sour to worried. "He says I've made so much progress with the tuberculosis vaccines. And he couldn't stop telling people I was his new scientific discovery. His star pupil."

Ursula's eyes squinted and she put a hand on her stomach. "Have you ever thought that your professor wants something in exchange for his mentorship? He's a widower after all."

"You're...vile! How dare you say such things about the professor? He's been nothing but supportive and a perfect gentleman."

Ursula sighed theatrically. "Just be careful. I don't want anything bad to happen to you."

As if even worse things could happen to me than already have. Anna snorted. "Ursula, I appreciate your worries, but you haven't even met Professor Scherer. He's a wonderful man. You would like him, I know you would."

Ursula shook her head, arguing, "No. I wouldn't. I don't care how nice and gentlemanly he appears to be, he's still a Nazi."

"Not everyone who is a Nazi is evil," Anna said.

"Really? You can tell that to me after seeing what they are doing to people? What they did to our sister? To you?"

"The professor didn't do anything to Lotte or the other prisoners." Anna trembled with fury. Why couldn't Ursula see how her constant judgments colored her beliefs?

"But the people he affiliates himself with did. And he knows," Ursula said, seemingly out of breath.

"You're just jealous." Anna walked past Ursula towards the bathroom.

"Jealous? Of you?" Ursula asked incredulously, trailing after her.

"Yes. Because I'm finally about to fulfill my dream of becoming a scientist, while you're stuck in that awful job of yours." Anna slammed the door shut, locked it behind her, and stepped under the cold shower – they hadn't had hot water for months.

Twenty minutes later she stepped into the kitchen, where Ursula was preparing lunch.

"Ursula," she said to the back of her sister. "I'm sorry. I know you are worried about me, but can't you also be happy for me?"

Ursula turned around, her eyes full of misery. "I am. You know I will always support you, and I am proud of you, but you need to be careful. Please, be careful."

"Who needs to be careful?" Mutter had entered the kitchen and placed two bags with groceries on the table.

"We were talking about my work at the hospital," Anna answered, evading Mutter's glance.

"Why don't I believe you, Anna Klausen?" Mutter said while Ursula busied herself putting the meager results of hours of standing in queues into the pantry.

"Is this all you've got for the entire week?" Ursula asked.

Mutter cast her a glance that meant "I-know-what-you're-doing" and gave a deep sigh. "Unfortunately, yes. Thank God for the allotments and Lydia's packages from the farm." Since both sisters worked irregular shifts and long hours, their mother had taken the brunt of the tedious standing in queues to organize food.

Having raised four children, she'd never held a formal job, but lately she had started to exchange sewing work for food, coal, or basically anything that could be traded.

CHAPTER 14

Anna arrived at the Charité Monday morning and was setting out to prepare new bacterial cultures when Professor Scherer appeared in the laboratory, clad in a white lab coat.

"Fräulein Klausen, would you please accompany me to the Pediatric Clinic?" he asked.

"Of course, Professor, let me finish setting up this round of tuberculosis experiments," Anna answered, holding a pipette in her right hand as she dumped droplets onto the nutrient solution in a round bowl. She'd finally found a way to control the growth of the bacterium. Once finished, she blew a strand of hair from her forehead and glanced at the professor, who'd been observing her.

"I believe I'm this close," she said, putting her fingers half an inch apart, "to finalizing a vaccine that will not only slow down the growth of the, but contain it entirely."

"We'll soon find out," the professor answered and

watched her as she disinfected and dried her hands. "Let's go."

On the way out, she tossed her lab coat into a basket for washing and grabbed a clean one. One could never be careful enough. God forbid, if the highly infectious bacteria spread into the wild...

Since the tour on her first day of work she hadn't returned to the patient wards of the Charité. The head doctor was already waiting for them and Professor Scherer made the introductions.

"Doctor Bessau, this is Anna Klausen, the young woman I was telling you about. She has made marvelous progress finding a possible tuberculosis vaccine."

"Then let's have a look at your work." The doctor smiled and handed them each gloves and a surgical mask.

Anna looked slightly confused at the two men, but put on the gear and followed them through the gated gangway to the quarantine barracks. The excitement of something important loomed in the air, but with every step she took towards the quarantine barracks, her steps become more labored as if she was treading through quicksand. The two men walked ahead of her, talking about a medical diagnosis she did not quite understand.

On the other side, they stepped into a huge room and the sight that greeted her knocked Anna's breath from her lungs. Memories she'd buried deep down snaked back up her spine to attack her out of the blue, and she staggered.

Roughly thirty cots were in the shabby room, each one occupied by an emaciated child. Regardless of their age, all of them were strapped to their beds, wearing diapers and not much else. Some had obvious deformities, others showed the empty glance of imbeciles, but most of the children simply lay whimpering, howling, and coughing.

Anna put a hand over her mouth, oxygen not reaching her brain anymore. The air became thick, too heavy to breathe, and she fought the urge to rip the mask away in her struggle for oxygen.

"What is this?" she asked, the horror etched into her face.

"Imbeciles. Cripples. Worthless members of society. It's disgusting, since most of them can't even control their bowels," the doctor answered.

"I can see that, but what are they doing here?" Anna asked, unable to look away as a child around six years of age started violently coughing, until blood smeared his face and bed sheet. At the other end of the room, a nurse gave another child an injection, but she didn't even look up to see which one of her little patients was coughing so hard.

Anna grabbed a paper towel and walked over to clean the blood and mucus from the little boy's face. He kept coughing and howling, his eyes empty. The sound chilled Anna to her bones.

"A waste of effort; he'll probably die within a day," the doctor said. "He got the first lot of the vaccine you're working on."

Anna felt the ground swaying beneath her and opened her mouth. No words came out. It took her several tries before she found her voice. "The...the vaccine isn't completed," she stammered.

The doctor nodded. "And the only way we will ever know for sure whether it works or not is to test it on a person. Laboratory tests can only tell us so much."

"But, but…you're infecting these children with tuberculosis!" Anna said.

"Not children. Degenerates. They have previously been selected for removal from society," the doctor told her matter-of-factly.

Anna shook her head. It was so wrong. Just because a child was soft in the head or had a game leg didn't mean they should have their life arbitrarily ripped from them.

"Fräulein Klausen, I know this may look cruel at first sight," the professor said, entering the conversation, "but you have to remember that these subjects aren't normal children. They are sub-humans, more similar to a guinea pig or a rabbit than to our race."

Why wouldn't the ground stop moving? Anna grabbed onto the bars of one of the cots and fought the dizziness attacking her. She thought she'd seen the abyss of human cruelty in Ravensbrück, but this? "But they are suffering…" she managed to murmur.

The doctor looked at her, his dark eyes void of any compassion. "I agree with you. This is unfortunate. Very unfortunate. A person with a pure heart like you cannot stand to see even the lowest animal suffering. But we have to be rational here; sometimes sacrifices have to be made for the greater good. And wouldn't you rather have one of these subjects suffer for a short time, if it can help to save hundreds of thousands? Our soldiers, mothers, beloved children?"

Anna couldn't form an answer. For the remainder of the morning, she trudged silently behind the two men, her brain trying to come to terms with what she'd witnessed.

At the end of the ward round, Doctor Bessau led them

back through the gangway to the open part of the Pediatric Clinic. There she glimpsed mothers sitting at the beds of their children, trying to hide the worry etched into their faces.

"Fräulein Klausen, so far you have done outstanding work." Professor Scherer congratulated her on their way back to the laboratories. "I would think a promotion is appropriate as soon as we see positive results from the vaccine."

"A promotion?" she asked.

"Yes, as head of the vaccine team. I also thought of having you enroll into university on a part-time basis. I have great plans for your future." He smiled at her and added, "Please excuse me; I have a lunch engagement."

Then he was gone, leaving Anna standing at the entrance to the building that hosted the laboratories, dumbfounded. Her entire life she'd been dreaming about this. Enrolling in university. Becoming a biologist. Helping people with her work.

But right now it tasted stale. More than that, it tasted *wrong*.

She skipped lunch and instead buried herself in work. Work that caused suffering to innocent children. The bowl with the nutritional solution slipped from her hand and shattered into a million pieces.

Anna closed her eyes for a moment and then grabbed a broom and shovel to clean up the mess. When she'd swept up the shards and mopped the floor, she tucked an unruly strand of hair behind her ear. Leaning on the broom she sighed. *Sometimes a few have to suffer for the benefit of many.*

In this war, everyone had to make sacrifices. Tuberculosis was one of the scourges of mankind, and she might be holding the key in her hands to rid humanity of an insidious disease. Could she really throw away the chance to help millions because a few dimwits had to suffer?

CHAPTER 15

The gnawing guilt nagged Anna for the rest of the day. Every time she thought she had it beaten back, it returned with a vengeance. When Anna arrived home, Ursula and Mutter were preparing dinner.

"Hello, darling," Mutter said, peeling potatoes. "You look tired."

"Yes, it was a tough day," Anna answered and poured herself a glass of water. She needed to talk to someone about the events of the day. Normally the first person to set her moral compass straight would be her mother, but she couldn't tell her. Not today anyway. Mutter still believed Anna was working as a simple nurse at the Charité. No, today she didn't have the strength to confess that she was working as a research assistant, trying to find a tuberculosis vaccine.

"Everyone is tired these days," Mutter said, attacking the next potato. "Who can sleep well with all the air raids and spending the nights in those dreadful bunkers? I wish the bloody Englishman would drop a bomb on me and it was over!"

Surprised by Mutter's sudden outburst Anna all but dropped the glass in her hand. Before the war, even before Lotte disappeared, her mother had been the slumbering bedrock of their family. Pleading for help, Anna glanced at her sister, but Ursula simply sat on her chair, her eyes treacherously damp.

Anna didn't understand the world anymore. Mutter yelled. Ursula cried. She wouldn't be able to talk to either one of them about her doubts. She studied Ursula's face. Something was different. Thinner, but also more rounded. That didn't make sense. Anna shrugged, over the last weeks, every conversation with her sister had ended in arguments and yelling.

"Can I help?" Anna asked, and then put a pot with water on the stove to boil the potatoes.

After dinner, Anna glanced at the clock. "Peter will pick me up in a few minutes."

"Now? It'll be dark soon," Mutter objected.

"Don't worry. I used to walk at night all the time when I was working shifts in Moabit. Ursula still does," Anna answered. Ursula often worked irregular shifts in her job as prison guard. It was the perfect cover for her activities in the underground network of Pfarrer Bernau and allowed her to leave the house at any time during day or night without raising suspicions.

"It's different now," Mutter said. "There's more crime with all those people not having enough food."

"Peter will walk me home," Anna assured her mother.

"How can I know he is a good man? You have not even presented him to me," Mutter said.

"You will get to know him. Soon. Just not today." It was a sore spot. Anna wished she could introduce him to her family, but she knew they wouldn't be fooled by his handsome looks. Mutter would discover on the spot that he was hiding something, and as long as Anna didn't know his secret, she didn't dare bring him home.

"That must be him," Ursula said as the doorbell rang.

Anna dashed down the stairs with a huge smile on her lips. When she opened the door, she threw herself into his arms.

"Wowza!" Peter echoed a word from some American film of so long ago. "What have I done to deserve this?" He chuckled and pressed a kiss on her cheek.

After walking hand in hand along the streets, they soon got tired of watching dust, rubble, and destruction.

"Want to come to my place to hear a radio show?" Peter asked. He lived in an apartment in one of the staff buildings at the Charité.

"That would be nice," Anna answered as they hopped onto a bus. While technically he had access to the professor's Mercedes at all times, he preferred not to use it during his off hours.

When they arrived at Peter's bachelor apartment, which consisted of a single bedroom, a bathroom, and a small kitchen that doubled as the sitting room, Anna's palms were moist.

Peter invited her to settle on the couch, and then turned on the radio before he made them hot tea and handed one mug to Anna.

"Would you mind waiting for a few minutes?" he asked with an apologetic expression. "I have to do some work."

"Surely. I won't run away." *Or maybe I will.* She had decided to talk to him about the things she saw this morning in the quarantine ward. But now she wasn't so sure revealing her true feelings was a great idea. She hadn't known him for a long time and he could be a spy, trying to find out what had really happened to her supposedly dead sister Lotte.

"It won't take long, sweetheart." He pressed a kiss on her cheeks, and inhaling his masculine scent made her throw all precaution overboard.

"Wait. I have to tell you something."

Peter's eyes darted between her and the closed bedroom door, where he kept his small desk.

"Please," Anna whispered. "It's important."

He pulled his chair to her side, and wrapped his strong arm around her shoulders. Anna took several deep breaths before she found the courage to expose the horrors of her guilt-ravaged mind. She took one look at Peter, and sucked in a ragged breath. Could she tell him what she'd seen?

"Professor Scherer took me to the Pediatric Clinic today. To the quarantine ward."

"He did?" Peter asked with a clenched jaw.

"I...it was awful. That vaccine I'm working on? I didn't know they were using the test sera to experiment on retarded children." She shuddered, the scenes of the morning flashing through her brain. "It was horrible."

Peter didn't say a word, just squeezed her shoulder. But his eyes betrayed no surprise.

"You knew?" she gasped.

"Since I'm not medical staff I've never been there, but yes, I always suspected something awful was going on back there," he answered, nudging her head to look at him. His radiant blue eyes had darkened. "You feel sorry for the children?"

"I do. This is wrong on so many levels. I wish they would stop!" Anna cried, holding his gaze.

"Talk to the professor. He listens to you more than anyone else I've ever known," Peter told her.

"Me? I'm only a research assistant."

"That's where you are wrong. Professor Scherer is convinced that you're brilliant. He's betting on you winning the Nobel Prize one day."

Anna shook her head. "It's not even him conducting the experiments, but Doctor Bessau, the head of the Pediatric Clinic. Even if I convinced the professor to let me stop preparing the bacterial cultures, it would make no difference. Someone else would do them. It's not that difficult, you know?"

"But it would make a difference for you," Peter insisted.

"It's not my fault! I'm just working in the laboratory, doing what I'm told to do. It's not me who's infecting children with a deadly disease! I didn't even know someone was testing the vaccines on humans!" Anna growled.

"But now you know. Will that change anything?" Peter folded his big hands across hers, as if to make sure she wouldn't balk.

"Holy hell! You're making it sound as if I'm the bad person here! I never wanted to experience any of this madness, I only worked in Ravensbrück to save..." Anna slapped a hand over her mouth, petrified at continuing the sentence. Even if her initial revelation hadn't caused Peter to turn away from her, she couldn't trust him enough to say more. To say it all. "...My work is going to make a difference one day. I can save thousands. Hundreds of thousands even. This vaccine might be able to eradicate one of the scourges of mankind. Don't you think that's worth something?"

"Anna, my sweet little Anna. I'm sure you have the best intentions, and the work you are doing will make a difference one day. But surely there must be another way to get the same result." Peter stroked her hair as he crooned the soothing words.

"I don't know what I can do..." She took a breath and then shook her head. Her mind reeled with the implications. Everywhere she turned, she found no rational answer. "Flat-out refusing to work on the bacterial cultures will ruin my career. Professor Scherer promised to promote me as soon as we see a success."

Peter took her face into both hands and locked eyes with her. "Sometimes sacrifices have to be made for the greater good."

CHAPTER 16

Anna had been putting in more and more hours at the Charité in a frantic quest to make that vaccine work as soon as possible. It was the only way she could think of to appease her conscience. Day in, day out she told herself that it wasn't her infecting the children, that she was merely growing the bacteria cultures, following orders. There was nothing she could do.

Sacrifices have to be made for the greater good. The words kept reverberating through her brain. Both Professor Scherer and Peter had used the same words, but their meaning lay worlds apart.

Anna shrugged and looked out the window. At this time of the year, March, spring should be on its way to light up the city. But instead of blossoming trees, flowers, and green grass, all she saw was ruins, rubble, and dead trees reaching their bare branches into the sky like the gnarled fingers of cursed creatures.

As if the daily fight to find food on the empty shelves

wasn't enough, the Allies had further increased the frequency of their air raids over Berlin. It wasn't only the Englishmen anymore that hung low in the skies dropping their deadly cargo, but also the Americans.

The radio news still talked about the awful losses the enemy had to suck up, and celebrated each downed hostile aircraft. But the Allies replaced every destroyed bomber with two new ones like the Hydra growing new heads. Anna shook a fist into the air.

Mutter's worry increased when Anna and Ursula walked the streets alone at night. But since that fateful day in the quarantine ward, Anna couldn't look her family in the eyes. It was one more reason why she stayed in her laboratory working as long as she could.

She wished she had a place to live on her own, where she didn't have to dodge the scrutinizing glance of her mother or the erratic mood swings of her sister. Sometimes on her way home, when she'd once again missed the last bus, she would even secretly wish to be hit by a bomb or killed by a random criminal; at least then her nagging conscience would be silenced forever.

That evening, when only she remained in the laboratory, she heard heavy footsteps in the hallway. Professor Scherer, clad in his greatcoat and a hat, opened the door and peeked inside saying, "I saw light in here. You are still working, Fräulein Klausen?"

"Yes, I just need to finish this one experiment, and then I'll leave for home."

He looked at her with the same disapproving glance Mutter used and said, "It's dangerous for a young lady out at this time of night. Our enemies don't give us any respite."

"I know, Professor, but I listened to the radio. So far they haven't announced any aircraft in German airspace heading for Berlin. And I'll be leaving in less than an hour."

He didn't look convinced and sat down on a high chair to observe her work. After several minutes he said, "I will wait for you to finish and bring you home in my car."

"Thank you." Anna smiled at the unexpected opportunity to see Peter. They hadn't made their relationship official yet, but she suspected that the Professor must have his suspicions.

Later when they sat in his limousine, Peter in the driver's seat and she and the Professor in the backseat, Professor Scherer leaned over and said, "I have thought about this. Most of the research staff lives on-site. I would have offered you one of the rooms, but with all the destruction, we've had to take on so many bombed-out relatives of our employees...nevertheless, I hate to see you walking alone at night."

"It's no problem, really..." Anna had no idea where this was going.

"Well, it is. I would never forgive myself if something happened to you. Therefore, I want you to consider living in my apartment at the Charité. I never use it...I prefer my house in Oranienburg or the one closer to Ravensbrück."

"Professor, that is a very generous offer..." *One I can't possibly accept.*

"No, it is an offer that should have been made long before now. I will make it official with our personnel department tomorrow morning." Professor Scherer leaned back in his seat, obviously satisfied with the solution he'd arrived at.

"I...I would love to." Anna's heart jumped at the idea of escaping the scrutiny of her family, and being closer to Peter, but she couldn't make such an important decision on her own. "But I must discuss this with my mother first."

"Very well. Surely your mother will see the advantage of your living on-site and not having to make the dangerous journey back to your home every night."

"Thank you again," she said as the automobile stopped in front of her curb. Peter glanced at her in the rearview mirror and she could see that he wanted to kiss her as badly as she wanted to kiss him. But in the Professor's presence, that wouldn't happen.

"Good night, Professor," she said and took Peter's hand.

He'd already walked around the automobile to help her out. For a long moment her hand lingered in his, and she wished she could wrap her arms around him. Instead she said, "Thank you, Peter. Have a good night."

Then she walked up to the apartment she shared with her mother and sister. It used to be quite crowded with a family of six, but now with only the three of them living there it felt big. Mutter occupied one bedroom, while Ursula and Anna shared the other one. A living room, separate kitchen, and private bathroom were luxuries not many still owned these days. Despite the government's efforts to evacuate as many non-essential citizens from Berlin as possible, there were still too many people remaining for the daily-shrinking stock of intact buildings.

She would miss her family. But she longed for independence.

"Mutter. Ursula." Anna rushed inside, still pondering how to break the news.

"You look excited, Anna. What is it?" Mutter asked, motioning for Anna to join them at the kitchen table.

"Well, you know how you've been worried about my safety when I had to walk home in the blackout?"

"I still do, darling. I worry every time one of you is out there," Mutter said, and poured potato soup into Anna's bowl.

"Then you will see the merits of this." Anna took a deep breath and said, "Professor Scherer has graciously offered me the use of his apartment at the Charité. Isn't that wonderful news?"

"He has asked you to live with him?" her mother asked, her face covered in a twisted mask of outrage.

"No, oh no. He never uses the apartment and it's sitting there vacant."

Her mother shook her head arguing, "Still, the apartment is his. How would it look? My daughter living in the apartment of a widowed man who could be her father. Over my dead body."

"Please, Mutter. It will be arranged with the personnel department and officially assigned to my name." Anna shot an unspoken plea to Ursula for help, and was amazed when she received it.

"Mutter, such arrangements are very common. We have employee housing on the prison grounds, too. There's nothing improper about it if it's done via the personnel department."

Mutter looked from Anna to Ursula and back. "I don't know…"

"You have to think about what's best for Anna. Walking home in the dark is dangerous and our enemies are unpredictable. Sometimes we have short notice in an air raid warning. If she lives on-site, you wouldn't have to worry about her being out so late."

"You'll still get to see me, because I'll come home anytime I get a chance. You'll even grow sick of my visits," Anna added.

"I don't like it," Mutter stated, but Anna could see her softening towards the idea.

"Please. It's not that I haven't lived on my own before," Anna said

"Don't mention that! I'm still angry with both of you about that ploy. You could have gotten all three of you killed." Mutter scowled at her and shook her head. "And don't believe for one minute that I haven't figured out what you're really doing at the Charité. *Nurse* Anna!"

"You know?" Ursula and Anna said in unison.

"A mother knows everything where her children are concerned. I may be getting old but I'm not stupid. I knew Lotte would get herself into trouble the same way I knew that you would never give up on your dream to become a biologist." Mutter curved her lip up into half a smile. "And I also know why Ursula has developed her religious streak recently and her sudden love for the allotment gardens."

"Why...why didn't you say anything?" Anna asked.

"Sometimes it's better to keep silent. And since you will move to the employee housing whether I agree or not, I hereby give you my blessing."

"Thank you, Mutter." Anna was moved to tears. She had expected to be scolded, but not this.

"Good night," Mutter said, and retreated to her bedroom.

"It's hard for her too, you know?" Ursula said when only the two of them remained in the kitchen. "She has no idea where Vater is being held captive, and now that she knows Richard is in Warsaw she listens to every bit of news coming in about Poland. I see her blanch whenever there's talk about an attack by the partisans or other troublesome information."

Anna vaguely remembered Peter's reaction to the murder of an SS officer in Warsaw. *Maybe he has a brother stationed in Poland, too?*

"Did you tell her? I mean about your work for Pfarrer Bernau's resistance network?" Anna asked.

"Of course not. We don't talk about these things. Ever. But how could she not notice when I hide Jews in our allotment garden? How food from the pantry is missing? We now have a secret sign to let her know when she can't visit the allotments."

For a moment Anna felt like scum. Ursula risked her life everyday to smuggle Jews out of the country, Lotte had paid the price for helping a friend.

And what do I do? Nothing.

"I should go pack," Anna said. "Professor Scherer has offered to arrange things first thing in the morning."

"I'll help you – if you'd like?" Ursula offered.

Anna smiled and squeezed her sister's hand, replying, "I'd like that very much."

They folded clothing, packed books and Anna's personal items, and placed them into the same suitcase she'd used to move to Ravensbrück.

"I hope this move will be happier for you," Ursula said and burst into tears.

"Sisterheart, don't cry." Anna put down the shirt she was folding and hugged her sister tight.

"I can't help it," Ursula sobbed, frightening the hell out of Anna. Her sister believed in staying strong and accepting what fate handed her. Ursula hadn't even cried after getting the news about her husband's death. So why had she become a crybaby lately?

"I'm not moving that far away." Anna hugged her tighter. How could Ursula be so upset that she was moving out? After a while the sobs faded, and Anna released her sister and stepped back to look her over.

Ursula nodded and tried to dry her tears. Anna watched her for a long moment, and when Ursula turned sideways to reach for another shirt to fold, Anna couldn't believe her eyes. There, hidden beneath the untucked shirt her sister wore, was an unmistakable bulge.

Anna sank back onto the bed and grabbed her sister's arm. "Why didn't you tell me?"

"Tell you what?" Ursula turned and looked at her cautiously.

"That you're pregnant!"

"I…" Ursula shrugged and burst into tears once more.

A troublesome suspicion settled like lead around Anna's heart. "Who is the father?"

"You know him." Ursula broke out into another round of violent sobs. "It's Tom."

"The English pilot? Oh my God!" Anna flung herself onto her back.

"Shush! You can't tell a soul." Ursula's panic-stricken eyes widened.

"I know that." Of course she knew. Tom Westlake was an

English pilot. The enemy. A convicted spy with a death sentence hanging over his head. A prison escapee. A hunted man accused of multiple crimes. The Gestapo was probably still looking for him, and if they suspected that Ursula's baby was Tom's…she didn't want to imagine what that would mean for all of them. Ravensbrück was a piece of cake compared to what the Gestapo had in store for their prisoners.

"Promise me, Anna. Nobody can know who the father is," Ursula begged.

"My lips are sealed." Anna raised her hand to her mouth and made a gesture as if she was turning a key and throwing it away, just as they'd done as children.

Ursula giggled, but sobered immediately. "I'm serious."

"Me too. Do you think I want to be on the other side of the fence in one of the camps even for one minute? God forbid. Your secret is safe with me." Anna did a quick calculation and figured her sister was in her sixth month. "Why didn't you come to me earlier?"

Ursula grimaced, saying, "Because you've been so occupied with your career, that professor, and Peter."

"Ursula, you are my family. I will never be too busy for you or…Mutter! Does she know?"

"No, and I want to keep it that way."

"For how long do you think you can conceal your condition?" Anna said after a glance at Ursula's growing belly. Now that she knew, the obvious pieces fell into place and everything made sense. The round face. The mood swings. The full breasts. "She'll find out soon if she doesn't know already." Ursula's eyes started watering again and Anna wished she'd kept quiet.

"It's just...you remember how I always wanted to have a child? I had it all worked out. I married Andreas, he would come home on furlough, and I'd bear his child. I could stop working in my awful job as prison guard and would stay home with our baby. When the war was over, we'd be a happy family."

Anna couldn't help but grin at the rosy picture her sister painted. Things hadn't worked out as planned for any of them. Not even for herself. She sighed, wondering at the course of her life if things had unfolded in a different way.

"I hear you. It's not that I had envisioned all this." Anna made an all-encompassing gesture and propped herself on her elbows. "But sometimes we have to accept what fate hands us, and make the best of it."

"Hey, that's my line." Ursula punched her sister's arm. Then a sad cloud crossed her eyes again. "I don't even know whether Tom made it back to England, or if he's still alive." She put a hand over her belly. "Every night when the bombers come, I look up into the sky, hoping to see him there." Tears fell again. "It's stupid; I know."

"It's not stupid. You love him," Anna said and snuggled against her sister's back.

"What if he falls in love with an English girl over there? He doesn't even know..." Ursula wiped her tears away and stood up. "I hate Hitler and I hate his war! Once it's over, there will be nothing left for the winner to take. There will only be scorched earth and dead bodies."

"We must have faith that there will be an end to this soon, and a better future for everyone." Anna attempted to calm her sister. "Let's get some sleep."

Secretly, she admired Ursula for being so strong. She

was small and thin, and her soft smile could fool anyone, but deep inside she had the unyielding strength of a steel fortress. Anna wondered if she would be able to love as unconditionally as Ursula did, sticking around for a man who was the enemy. Thankfully, she didn't have to find an answer to this question. Her life was complicated enough as it was.

CHAPTER 17

Anna moved into her new place the next day. Because the apartment had previously been assigned to Professor Scherer, it was nicer than the usual staff quarters. It featured two bedrooms, one of which she didn't use, a combination living and dining room, and a fully furnished kitchen. Best of all, it was less than five minutes' walk to the lecture hall with the laboratories, and Peter lived in the adjacent building.

But in the midst of her happiness, a smidgeon of guilt gnawed at her over leaving her family when they needed her most.

Anna shrugged. It had been the right choice. She glanced at the clock on the wall opposite her work station and yawned. It was past nine p.m. already. Now that she could work as long as she wanted without having to worry about walking home in the pitch black of night, she'd forgotten the time again.

Usually Peter dropped in to remind her about dinner-time and they would prepare a meal either at her place or at his, but today he'd been out driving the Professor to several appointments.

Everyone else had already left. She stretched her arms and legs, tidying up everything and locking the bacteria cultures into the cupboard. Then she grabbed her coat and purse, switched off the lights, and turned towards the stairs that would lead her straight out to the street side of the building.

The chilly night air smelled of fresh beginnings. Spring had finally returned to Berlin. Dandelions and daisies had sprung up everywhere, even atop heaps of rubble, as if to say *Look! We don't care whether there's a war or not, we'll always be here.*

Anna smiled and picked a bunch of daisies to put into a vase. Peter would like that. He always tried to cheer her up, bringing normalcy into her life, even if only with a flower. Moments later the screeching, buzzing, deafening sound of the air raid sirens blasted out across the city.

After so many years she should have grown accustomed to it, but every time it made her writhe in agony – like the sound of nails screeching across a blackboard, only a hundred times louder. Anna looked around for her options. The public shelter was on the far end of the grounds, at least a fifteen-minute walk. But there was a smaller one, nothing more than a fortified room in the basement of the lecture hall. She dreaded spending the night there. She hated that tiny room.

The deep droning of approaching aircraft drowned out even the sounds of the sirens and she knew she didn't have a choice. She'd never make it to the public shelter.

She hurried down the stairs, trying to contain her fear at entering the creepy space in the basement. There was only a dim emergency light blanketing the room in semidarkness.

"Iiieeeekkk," she shrieked when she noticed a shadow looming in the room.

"Is that you, Anna? It's me. Peter," he called to her from the darkness.

"Jesus, Peter, you spooked me. I thought…" Anna fell into his arms, her heart pounding hard and fast.

"…I was a ghost? Boooo…" He chuckled at the trembles running down her arms. "You're safe with me. I'll take good care of you."

The sounds overhead grew louder, more terrifying, a swarm of angry hornets zooming in on their target.

"I hate them," she murmured.

"Everyone does. But they're just doing their job."

"How can you say that!" Anna turned in his arms, glaring daggers at him. "They're killing innocent people. Why don't they bomb military targets? Why do they come here to murder innocent women and children?"

"There are no innocents in a war. Not in this one." His voice became thoughtful and reminded her of her own inner struggles.

"Can we talk about something else, something less depressing?" Anna asked in a hushed voice as she leaned into him again. In his arms she felt safe. Nothing could harm her.

"Certainly, what do you want to talk about?" Peter chuckled again, tracing lazy circles on her arms. It felt so good. Too good. Her body threatened to ignite as she waited with bated breath for whatever he would do next.

"Tell me about your life before the war. Before you worked for the professor," Anna said.

"There's not much to tell."

"Please," she begged, snuggling up against him, feeling the warmth of his body enveloping her like a plush blanket.

"Well. I grew up on a farm in the middle of nowhere. I'm the oldest of four and after finishing school all I wanted was to escape. Life in the capital seemed so much more exciting." He chuckled again, snuggling her close. "For a while my life was perfect, but then the war happened. And now I'm here working for Professor Scherer."

Anna leaned her head back against him. His words had left her with more questions than answers, but as his fingers lightly traced the skin on her neck, her brain refused any rational thought. Tucked into his arms, her body seemed to burn up with need.

Peter shifted her around on his lap, so she faced him, and tipped her chin up to place a kiss on her lips. Shudders of delight raced through her veins, tingling sensations spreading all the way into her toes.

Anna opened her lips and his tongue slid inside, exploring her mouth, sending more sweet tingles across her body. His hands slid down her ribcage, pulling at her blouse, and then she felt his rough palms on her soft skin. Delicious prickles made her shiver and moan with delight – until the images of T the devil taking what she didn't want to give attacked her and she frantically pushed against Peter's chest.

"Anna, what's wrong?" Peter groaned, breathless.

"Nothing. I thought I heard an explosion." She hopped from his lap and walked towards the door. He followed her and put a hand on her shoulder. She jumped.

"My sweet Anna. What's going on? Are you afraid of me?" he said with a controlled voice, trying his best to stay calm.

"No." Anna shook her head, but one glance at Peter's face told her he didn't believe one word. "Not of you."

"What scares you so much that you run away every time I kiss you?"

She couldn't possibly answer. He would despise her if he knew the truth, he might even break up with her. The prospect of never seeing him again made her mouth go dry as cotton balls.

"Just hold me, please," Anna finally said.

Peter didn't respond, but pulled her against his chest and wrapped both arms around her, resting his chin upon the top of her head. Impact after impact shook the building above them and the ground vibrated with each new explosion.

"Close your eyes and try to relax. We'll most likely be down here the rest of the night," Peter said and carried her over to one of the cots, where he laid her down, and then squeezed in behind her, holding her tight. He covered them both with a blanket and while the apocalyptic inferno raged outside, shaking the earth with the wrath of a giant, Anna jittered, trembled, and prayed to survive this night.

Despite the never-ending bombing, she must have dozed off in the security of Peter's arms, because she woke with a start in the middle of the night, disorientated. Another forceful hit nearby moved the ground like Jell-O, and fear sank deeper into her bones. The emergency lights had stopped working and in the complete darkness, she sensed Peter's chest going up and down with his breath. He seemed fast asleep, but at the sound of the next explosion he jumped and muttered, *Cholera, wszyscy tu zginiemy.*

Cold hands grabbed at her heart as she remembered where she'd heard this expression before. Some of the Polish prisoners at Ravensbrück had used it and it roughly translated to *Damn, they're going to kill all of us.*

She squinted her eyes at him, more divining his features than seeing them. With his dirty blond hair and bright blue eyes he didn't look like a Pole. Not like the ones she knew anyways. He couldn't be a Pole. They belonged to the defamed Slavic race, and relationships between Aryans and Slavs were strictly forbidden. *There must be a perfectly valid reason for him to mutter in Polish in his sleep.* She'd confront him in the morning.

CHAPTER 18

The next morning, Anna and Peter awoke and surveyed the shelter to make sure it had survived the bombings intact. Peter opened the steel door and a cloud of dust entered.

Anna coughed and held on to Peter's hips when she peeked out at the picture of destruction. Despite being in the basement, she could see into the blue sky. Part of the building had crumbled and the stairs were covered with debris.

"That looks bad. You stay behind me," he said, and began moving bricks, wood, and pieces of concrete from the entrance until he and Anna could emerge from the small shelter. Sunshine filtered through the hole in the roof as he took her hand. "Quick, we don't know how long this is going to hold up."

Anna wrapped her scarf over mouth and nose to avoid breathing in dust and smoke. But the thin veil couldn't hinder the distinctive smell of burnt human flesh that filled her nostrils. She choked. In contrast to the cremated bodies of Ravensbrück these unfortunate people had probably burnt alive.

A typical air raid consisted of explosive bombs first, mines second. The destructive force of their detonation waves blew through stone walls as if they were nothing more than paper. Phosphor bombs came last. The ensuing fire found more than enough nutrition in wooden furniture exposed by shattered walls to rage through the city long after the bombers had gone.

It was a sequence designed for maximum destruction. In this war everything was permitted. Neither side held back anymore, and civilians were as much targets as soldiers or military bases, unlike in the Great War just twenty years prior.

As they ascended to the open ground, the full extent of the damage caused Anna to gasp. Several buildings had sustained massive damage; the formerly beautiful red brick houses were merely ruins. Hospital beds and medical equipment littered the ground like toy blocks in a nursery. Wounded patients filled the air with their whining and whimpers.

Several nurses and other staff frantically tried to dig up entombed patients with their bare hands. Anna and Peter jumped in to help, moving brick after brick until yet another howling person could be freed, and carried on a stretcher to a safe area where volunteers had set up a makeshift hospital tent.

Anna's soul wept with each new victim they unearthed. They found two children embracing each other, their angelical faces directed upwards. After Anna closed their eyes and crossed them off the list of missing persons, she staggered and sat on a pile of debris.

"I can't do this anymore," she murmured.

"Yes you can," Peter encouraged her, touching her shoulder.

She gave a bitter laugh. In reality, what choice did she have but to carry on? Everyone in Berlin lived in constant fear, praying to survive another day. If they had known how bad things would become, would they still have willingly followed Hitler into this cataclysmic war?

Much later in the day, Professor Scherer organized an all-hands meeting in the mostly unscathed lecture hall. There had been casualties mostly amongst the nurses on night shift, but also three members of Anna's research team, including the team leader, had been confirmed dead. The professor tried to instill the power of endurance and motivation into his staff, but everyone left the meeting with long, somber faces.

"Fräulein Klausen, a word," he called after her as she left with the crowd.

"Yes, Professor Scherer." Anna turned to watch the man whom she'd admired since her childhood. She still thought his scientific work was outstanding, but she'd also seen the dark side of him. She pushed the thoughts away. Since that day at the quarantine ward, she'd done her best not to think of the suffering children – and her role in it. She'd convinced herself that she couldn't change a thing. It didn't matter who was growing the bacterial cultures. If it weren't her, someone else would take her place.

And perhaps the greater good did justify such a sacrifice?

"How are you holding up?" the professor asked.

"Like everyone else, I'm shaken. But I'll be fine. There's no other choice than to carry on."

He raised his brows at her. "I'm glad you're taking this torment with such dignity. In dire times we come to value the strength of leaders."

Anna had no idea where he was going with this, but his next sentences had her hiss in a puff of air.

"As you know, your team leader perished last night and we are in need of a replacement. It is not the promotion I had in mind for you, but the position is yours nonetheless."

"Me? You want me to head up the research team?" Anna asked, incredulous. She'd be in charge of a team of scientific assistants, all taking their direction and orders from her. It was the culmination of her career aspirations. "I'm honored."

"You'll make a fine leader. Your duties will be expanding, but I know you'll handle your extra responsibility just like you handle everything else. With poise and a sharp mind," the professor assured her.

"Thank you. Can you give me some guidance about my additional duties?" Anna asked.

"Don't worry. Doctor Schmid will guide you every step of the way. He'll be happy to have you as one of the team leaders." With these words the professor dismissed her. Doctor Schmid was the chief of bacteriology research and also held a position as doctor in the Pediatric Clinic. Anna thought he was a good scientist, driven by ambition, but a much worse superior, because he lacked understanding of interpersonal relationships.

The next day Doctor Schmid explained to her that she

would have to continue her work in the laboratory, due to lack of a replacement for her, but in addition she had to work on a more strategic level, proposing new lines of experiments.

Anna beamed at him, barely able to believe her own ears. She was tasked with thinking up, creating, directing, and analyzing an experiment from beginning to end. It was everything she'd hoped for and more.

She would prove worthy of Professor Scherer's trust and help develop cures for the most devastating diseases of mankind. She already imagined herself in the company of Marie Curie and Irène Joliot-Curie, who'd been the only two women ever to receive a Nobel Prize outside of the categories Literature or Peace.

CHAPTER 19

It seemed like Anna worked around the clock since Professor Scherer had promoted her. Driven by the need to succeed, she didn't mind that her social life had been reduced to zero. It wasn't like there were many fun things to do anyways. Since Stalingrad a year ago there had been more or less a permanent ban on dancing. Approved motion pictures were usually disguised propaganda, and one never knew if the favorite restaurant would still be standing the next day.

Due to her workload, she hadn't visited Mutter and Ursula for an entire week, and even going out with Peter had taken a backseat to her work. On the one hand she longed to spend more time with him, but on the other hand she knew she'd have to confront her inner demons first, should she spend more time with him. He wouldn't stay content with a kiss here and there forever.

The clock on the wall ticked loudly in the otherwise

silent laboratory. After having dinner with Peter, she'd returned to her work station to finish just *one more* analysis. Suddenly the shrill noise of a ringing phone disturbed her train of thought.

She eyed the black apparatus, wondering who could be calling at this time of night. All the other employees had already gone home. Sighing, she picked up the receiver, expecting to hear the voice of one of the doctors in charge.

"Anna Klausen," she answered the telephone.

"This is Alexandra."

Alexandra? I don't know anyone called Alexandra. Then her tired brain clicked and put a face to the voice. Her sister Lotte. Oh yes, she lived now under the false name of Alexandra Wagner.

"Is everything alright?" Anna asked, wondering how Lotte had gotten her number.

"Your sister Ursula gave me your number. I hope it's okay," Lotte said.

"Yes. Usually we are advised not to use this line for private calls, but I guess since it's way past ten o'clock, it's fine. How are you? Are you getting enough to eat?"

Lotte sighed, saying, "Enough is relative. But I'm gaining weight if that's what you're worried about."

"Now, tell me why you're calling." Anna knew her sister didn't make social calls.

"I need a favor," Lotte said.

"Tell me." Anna's heart froze over. Knowing her sister, she knew she wouldn't like what would come next.

"Please promise to listen first, will you?"

"Fine." Anna was now sure she wouldn't like the favor her sister was asking for.

"I applied to become a *Wehrmachtshelferin* and be trained as a radio operator. But since I don't have family to vouch for me, I need a recommendation. Preferably from a well-respected person who has a high standing with the Party. Someone like Professor Scherer."

"But...you can't become an assistant to the Wehrmacht unless you're eighteen."

"You forgot my birthday!" Lotte said with mock indignation. "I turned eighteen last month."

"What?" Last time Anna checked, Lotte's birthday was in September. "Sorry, I forgot. Belated congratulations." Anna held up the charade just in case the line was tapped. But she cursed Ursula for making Lotte seven months older in her false papers. She should have made her not one, but five years younger to keep her out of trouble.

"You still there, Anna?"

"Yes...Alexandra. Are you sure you want this? Radio operators follow the front line, helping the war effort by gathering information and sending it to headquarters...oh dear...don't tell me this is your plan! It's too dangerous!" Anna gasped. Knowing Lotte's hatred for the Nazis, this could only mean one thing. She wanted to work as a spy for the Allies and send them secret information.

"That is exactly my plan! Anything to shorten this war. We all have to chip in and do our share. Isn't that what our *Führer* says?" Lotte spat out the words, and Anna could clearly hear their true meaning.

"It's suicide. Wouldn't your mother rather see you safe at home?" Anna argued, trying to convince her sister.

"I don't have family left. They all perished in the air raid over Cologne two years ago." Lotte was recounting her cover story. Again, Anna cursed Ursula. She should have made Lotte a stupid farm girl with ten siblings she couldn't leave alone. Not an orphaned girl fending for herself.

"What if the enemy captures you and sends you to a prisoner-of-war camp?" Maybe the memory of her time in Ravensbrück would change Lotte's mind.

"Can't scare me. I want to help rescue what is left of my beloved Germany. Now will you help me, please?" Lotte begged.

"Stubborn as a mule, why does that remind me of my dead sister?" Anna murmured and then sighed. "Since I'm sure you won't give up on this idea, I'll see what I can do. But I won't make any promises."

"Thank you. You're the best friend anyone could ever ask for. Anna…" Lotte paused and Anna could hear the unmistakable effort to hold back tears. "That doctor…did he? After that day…" Lotte couldn't complete her sentence.

Anna clenched her hand around the phone receiver. Clearly, Lotte was blaming herself for the abuse Anna had had to suffer at Doctor Tretter's hands. Anna closed her eyes and then forced her voice to remain even as she lied. "Just that one time."

"Oh, Anna! I was so afraid…"

"That's all in the past," Anna said, unwilling to delve into that painful memory.

"We need to move on, every one of us," Lotte whispered into the phone.

Anna finished the conversation, thinking that each of the sisters had her own burden to carry. Lotte had suffered immeasurable evil, and yet she had jumped right back on her feet, willing to do whatever it took to rid her country of its nefarious government.

Anna tidied up her workplace, guilt spreading through her. Both of her sisters were so much more valiant and upright than she was. Ursula risked her life every day to smuggle Jews out of the country and Lotte wanted to become a spy. Either one would be hanged as traitor should she ever be exposed.

And what am I doing?

She grabbed her coat and switched off the lights in the laboratory. A tepid breeze greeted her as she stepped out of the building. After this long and hard winter, everyone in Berlin embraced the coming spring. It was a promise of new beginnings, of another chance at life.

Not for everyone, though. Not for the poor children used as guinea pigs.

I'm just following orders. There's nothing I can do to help these children. It wouldn't make a difference for them if I stopped.

Anna's stomach churned and she walked faster. Within two minutes she stood in front of the entrance to the employee housing. She turned around and walked past the lecture hall and the Pediatric Clinic, to the far end of the campus where the makeshift tent-hospital stood.

Moaning, whining, and screams of pain cut through the air like knifes. On top of being sick and wounded, the patients were in danger of contracting an infectious disease like typhus, cholera … or tuberculosis.

You're doing the right thing. This vaccine can save so many people.

Millions were dying in this war; what difference did a few handicapped children make? Deep down she knew it was wrong, but she brushed it away, preferring to listen to the voice of reason. The voice that said the end justified the means. In war, everyone had to do things they wouldn't do under normal circumstances. Soldiers had to kill.

And she had to accept unintended side effects of her research.

CHAPTER 20

Anna put on the black two-piece outfit she'd bought with Doctor Tretter's ration cards. Despite her hatred for the man, she couldn't afford not to use the single elegant dress suit she possessed.

Professor Scherer had been invited to a social event at the home of the Minister of Science, and had asked Anna to accompany him. As usual, Peter would drive them; Anna waited for the Mercedes to round the corner.

When the limousine stopped in front of her and Peter jumped out to hold the door open for her, her heart leaped. He looked so incredibly handsome in his black uniform suit. A roving glance accessed her body, and an appraising smile lit up his eyes. Everywhere his eyes touched, Anna burned with a smoldering heat.

"You look swell today," he said as he helped her into the backseat. Her stomach somersaulted as she slid in next to the professor.

"Fräulein Klausen, I'm so glad you found the time to be

my companion. If you impress the Minister as much as you impressed me with your intelligence and your charm, there won't be a limit to what you can achieve," Professor Scherer said.

"Of course, Professor." Anna nodded her agreement. She had learned that making a career in science involved as much social mingling and impressing the right kind of people as it involved actual work in the laboratory.

"Be careful what kind of information you divulge, Fräulein Klausen. We don't want to put all our cards on the table at once and we definitely don't want Professor Lugauer from Munich listening in and duplicating our research work," the professor briefed her.

Anna listened carefully and nodded as Peter drove them past the destroyed center of Berlin.

"Where are we going?" she asked as Peter drove along the shore of Berlin's biggest lake, the Wannsee. This far outside of the city proper, the picture of destruction faded away and Anna almost forgot about the ugly war raging.

"Schwanenwerder Island," the professor said.

"Really?" Anna gasped. Schwanenwerder Island was the most prestigious location in Berlin. Nazi bluebloods like Joseph Goebbels, Hitler's personal physician Theo Morell, and the Minister of Armaments and War Production Albert Speer made their homes there. Ordinary mortals weren't granted access to the island.

Peter drove the Mercedes across the bridge that connected the island with the mainland and stopped in front of the gate.

Two uniformed SS men pointed their guns at them,

while a third one approached the car to check for their identification papers.

"Professor Scherer, welcome to Schwanenwerder Island," he said after the obligatory Heil Hitler and checking their invitation.

Anna's mouth went dry at the prospect of entering the home of the Minister of Science, but at the same time she was curious about his lifestyle. She'd already witnessed how the Nazi elite celebrated major accomplishments. It stunned her that while all of Berlin scrounged and skimped and stole to survive on the meager ration cards, the inner circle of power apparently didn't lack for anything.

"Professor, if I could ask a favor?" Anna murmured, her palms sweaty.

"Of course, Fräulein Klausen. What is it?"

"A friend of mine, her name is Alexandra Wagner and she wants to volunteer as radio operator to help the war effort."

"A noble cause, to be sure. We need more active young women like her," the professor commented.

"Alexandra is orphaned without close relatives and she asked me for a character reference," Anna said, hemming and hawing; "it's…she's a hard worker and I'm sure she would be an excellent addition to the war effort, but…well, I was wondering if you would be able to write one for her? A reference, that is. I mean your word holds so much more weight than mine."

"Our Führer needs every single person to do his share. I will gladly recommend her to help the total war. During this time where everyone has to chip in, how could I deny my support to a deserving young lady eager to volunteer?"

"Thank you so much." A sense of relief overcame her, and Anna sank back into the soft leather seat. She wasn't convinced she liked Lotte's plan to become a spy, but bull-headed as her sister was she'd find a way, and with Professor Scherer's recommendation she might be deployed to a less dangerous place. At least Anna hoped this would be the case.

"We're here," Peter announced as he pulled into the driveway of a huge mansion.

"Everyone is anxious to meet you, my newest scientific discovery," the professor said as they walked towards the entry door, Peter a few steps behind.

Throughout the evening Anna found herself being propelled around the room and introduced to so many people, there was no way she could remember all of their names. As always Peter kept a few steps behind the profes-sor. Anna doubted there was a real danger to the professor's life in the Minister's house, but she enjoyed feeling Peter's presence. It grounded her amidst all the important men in gala uniform with beautiful women hanging from their arms.

Waiters in livery flitted about, handing a glass of cham-pagne to the professor and another one to Anna. Out of the corner of her eye, she noticed how the waiter stopped in front of Peter, unsure whether to offer him one, too. But Peter shook his head.

"To your career," the professor said as they clinked glasses.

Anna smiled, sipping the sparkling drink and looking around at the opulence and luxury of the house. "This place is…so nice."

"The Minister does have great taste," someone commented. Another person pointed at one of the paintings saying, "This Rembrandt is a gift from Holland."

The smile on Anna's face froze over. Anyone knew how voluntary those *gifts* were. Usually the Nazis seized all valuables of their Jewish prisoners before handing them over to whatever fate they had planned for them. But also the churches, monasteries, museums, and art collections in the occupied zones had been persuaded to send treasured items *on loan* to the Reich.

As the evening wore on, the conversations turned to the one topic every single person in Europe was concerned about: the war.

"We cannot let this heinous attack on our livelihood remain unanswered," a general said. His uniform contained too many decorations to count.

"You can bet that's so. Hermann has his aces in readiness for a counterstrike," someone else answered. "The Allies will soon be wishing they'd never sent a single plane to Berlin."

Anna felt Peter moving closer to her, and when she casually looked around to catch his glance, she found him fixated on the conversation. *Why are men so interested in the details of how best to fight and kill?* She eventually tuned out the war talk and instead examined her surroundings and the people present. Everything seemed so normal and well put together. In this mansion it was as if the razed city didn't exist. Despair, hunger, and battered humanity – all this was far away from the opulence of the gathering.

"...she has been promoted to the position of research team leader."

Peter nudged her and he whispered over her shoulder,

"The professor is announcing your promotion. Pay attention."

Professor Scherer made a long pause and pushed Anna to the center of the room, before he clinked a spoon to his glass. The room grew silent and everyone turned their heads towards them. Anna felt her cheeks flush.

"Ladies and gentlemen, Minister: this young lady, Anna Klausen, has been doing exceptional work in my bacteriology research team. After the unfortunate demise of three of our staff members, she was promoted to research team leader. And now..." he glanced at her with excitement, "...in agreement with the Minister of Science, I have approved her enrollment to the studies of Genetics and Medicine at the Charité in addition to her work duty."

The crowd clapped their hands and Anna's head swirled. All she could do was hold herself upright and smile. Her dream was coming true right before her eyes.

"I know, this double duty hasn't been attempted before. And everyone in here knows the work involved, but, in truth, I'm not willing to let my best research assistant leave." He grinned, continuing, "I'm sure Fräulein Klausen will rise to the challenge."

"Thank you so much. I will not disappoint you," was all Anna could say.

An old man holding a monocle in front of his face approached them. "Professor Scherer, you place a lot of confidence in a mere woman. Where will this country end up if we need women to do men's work?"

Anna sent him a scowl. For the last four and a half years women had been doing the men's work to keep this country and its citizens alive. They worked in mills, on farms, in hospitals, in schools, in military factories, everywhere. They cleaned debris after air raids, rebuilt houses, paved roads, repaired Panzers. They did everything, because the men had left to kill other men.

"Great talents like Fräulein Klausen need to be promoted. During hard times and with our best men at the front, we must grab hold of greatness and nurture it, wherever it is to be found. Even in a woman."

The old man bowed his head and retreated. Then a long file of guests hurried to rub shoulders with her, if not to congratulate then at least to snatch up morsels of the esteem pouring over Anna. With every compliment Anna became a bit surer of herself, proud of her achievements and eager to continue on the path of her dream career.

Whatever stress came with her position, she'd handle it. Look at what she'd already handled in her young life! Sacrifice came in many forms, but for the greater good, she would do what was necessary.

CHAPTER 21

At the end of the long evening, Peter dropped off the professor at his residence in Oranienburg. Anna slipped into the front passenger seat, and then they made the long drive back to the Charité.

"Did you have a nice evening?" Peter asked, his eyes glued to the dark road.

"Yes. But it was also surreal."

"Surreal?"

"All the luxuries, the beautiful dresses, the jewelry of the women, the food, the champagne, while the rest of Berlin starves."

Silence hung between them until Peter raised his voice again. "I know. It feels so wrong – that I have such a good life, while my family struggles."

Anna turned her head, since it was the first time he'd mentioned his family. "You said you were raised on a farm? Shouldn't they be better off in the country? I know my Aunt

Lydia is. They have much more food than we do, since they can grow some themselves."

"It's complicated." Peter sighed. "One day after the war, I hope I can show you my home."

"That would be nice." Anna's heart fluttered, and she wished she could be more affectionate with him. She yearned to be in his arms, to kiss him, to feel his touch on her skin. But whenever they were alone together, and he tried to be more intimate, she froze up, unable to leave the memories of Doctor Tretter's abuse behind.

She gave a loud sigh, wishing things could be different. Peter didn't deserve her ice-cold responses when she wanted to thaw for him more than anything.

"What's wrong, my sweet Anna?" Peter asked and put a hand on her thigh. Anticipation coursed through her veins, and she made the decision that she would not let the lingering shadows of T the devil ruin her love for Peter. She wouldn't allow the past to control her future. Not any more.

"Nothing is wrong, but I thought it would be nice if you could stay at my place tonight," Anna said. There...she'd done it and said the words before she could take them back.

"Wow! That's unexpected," he said in a husky voice and she could hear his breathing speed up. "You sure about this?"

"Yes." Her voice reflected more confidence than she felt. Deep inside her stomach a knot of fear formed, ready to burst apart and flood her system with panic. But she needed to do this, if she ever wanted to be free.

He stopped the car for a moment and gazed at her. "Just know that I love you either way."

Anna nodded and raised her lips to receive his kiss. The

knot in her stomach still lingered, but being in Peter's arms felt too good, too safe to let the fear overtake her. When he released her mouth, she rubbed his scratchy beard and said, "I love you too, Herr Wolf."

"I have to stop at my place first," he said as he started the engine again. "It won't take long. Should I take you home and come by later?"

"No, I can wait for you in the automobile." Anna twisted her fingers.

When he pulled the Mercedes to a stop, he opened the door and then looked at her, tension rolling off of him, saying, "You sure you can wait here? I won't be long."

Anna nodded. It was rather unusual that he didn't invite her in to wait. He probably didn't want to make her walk up the three floors wearing her high heels. And she didn't mind a few moments to herself to bolster her courage for what she had planned.

The minutes rolled by and after fifteen minutes of sitting in the cold car, she began to wonder what was taking Peter so long. He must have forgotten the time working on something for the professor.

After five more minutes, she decided to check up on him. She knocked on the door, and when no answer came, worry attacked her. She turned the knob and the door sprang open, but the sitting room was empty and the bathroom door stood half open. That was more than a little worrisome, and her neck hair stood on end.

She should probably leave. But then she heard the sound of rhythmic tapping coming from behind his closed bedroom door.

"Peter?" she said, hesitantly. "Is that you?"

But no answer came. Her heart thumping furiously in her throat, she approached the bedroom door. The rhythmic tapping stopped for a moment and she closed her eyes. But then it started again.

Anna opened the door, and gasped when she saw Peter bent over a suitcase holding something that looked like a sophisticated radio, his forefingers feverishly hitting a switch. Peter jumped up, slamming the suitcase shut and drawing his Mauser. His eyes opened wide when he recognized her, and the hand with the pistol dropped to his side.

"What…what are you doing here?" he stammered.

"I got cold and tired of waiting. But I should ask what you are doing!" Anna barely kept herself from yelling at him.

"We need to talk," Peter said, and locked the suitcase before he pushed it behind the closet.

She nodded, her face ashen, and her previous plan of sleeping with him tonight flew from her mind as she considered the implications of what she'd just seen. "So this is what you've been hiding from me. Who the hell are you?"

"Anna, let's go into the other room and talk. I'll explain everything," he begged her.

Like a puppet on strings she returned to the front room, seating herself on the edge of the chair. "Explain!"

"My sweet Anna." He tried to take her hand into his, but she moved away. As her mind raced, his deception became bigger, turning into a raging giant. Had she not seen his betrayal with her own eyes, she'd never have believed it could be true.

"I was transmitting a message to London, warning them about the planned bombing that was discussed at the event."

He sighed, his eyes pleading with her to trust him. But how could she trust a man who'd deceived her about his true person? Who worked for the enemy?

"Why?" Anna whispered. She'd known he was not a fervent Nazi like so many others, but this? Her head ached with the revelation and the implications.

"I'm Polish. I escaped to Britain right after Hitler invaded and defeated our army. It was my duty to continue the fight to free my country." He bit down on his lower lip.

"You're a Pole – that explains it," Anna said, remembering the muttered words in his sleep. "And an English spy. Oh, I was so stupid." She hid her face between her hands. The man she had trusted, the man she had loved – a liar.

"Anna, I'm sorry you had to find out this way. I wanted to tell you, but I wasn't sure if..."

"If you could trust me?" she spat out the words. "The question is how I could ever think of trusting you? You're betraying my fatherland..." Sobs bubbled up in her chest and it took all her self-control to swallow them down.

"Will you call the Gestapo on me?" he asked, and she believed she saw him shiver with fear.

"No." She sighed, her confusing emotions making it hard to form a clear thought. "It's not so much what you did – still do – that bothers me, but that you never told me."

"Can you forgive me?" he asked, his eyes full of sadness.

"I don't know." She shrugged and stood. "I will go home now."

"I'll walk you–"

"No." Her voice was sharper than intended, but she needed to be alone. Away from the effect he had on her body.

"You're sure?" Peter searched her face and then sighed before nodding.

"Next time, lock the door," she said, and left his apartment without looking back.

The five-minute walk to her building wasn't nearly long enough to clear her thoughts, and she flopped down on the small couch, staring at the ceiling. Everything had become a whole lot more complicated.

She shouldn't be surprised. She'd always know that Peter was hiding a dark secret. But she'd also known that he was a good man, a man of integrity. He had no choice but to fight for his country. Fight against the Nazi evil.

Anna started bawling. It seemed everyone around her was involved in fighting the Nazis. Devout, obedient Ursula smuggled Jews out of the country, Lotte wanted to become a spy for the Allies, and Peter…he was a Polish soldier, and a spy.

And her?

She had the career she's always dreamed of, but her excitement over that epic achievement had dissolved like mist in the wind within the last hour. In the bigger picture, where things truly mattered, she was a complete and utter failure.

Not only didn't she oppose the regime that had brought terror and destruction to all of Europe, but she'd also become a spoke in their wheel. A puppet using her mind and gifts to their benefit.

How could I have let it come to this?

CHAPTER 22

The next morning Anna went to visit her family. She'd been so caught up in her new promotion and her career, it had been a while since she'd seen them. Despite still owning a key to the apartment, she preferred to ring the bell.

"Anna. Come in. What a nice surprise," Ursula greeted her as she opened the door.

Anna hugged her sister tight, and noticed how much bigger Ursula's stomach had grown. It wouldn't be long before she was unable to hide her growing belly beneath her untucked blouses.

"Does Mutter know yet?" Anna gestured to her sister's belly.

Ursula shook her head and led her sister over to the kitchen table. "Mutter is running errands. She should be back soon. Do you want some tea?"

"Thanks, tea would be fine." Mutter grew peppermint

plants in the allotment so they always had a fresh or dried supply of leaves for tea.

While Anna waited for Ursula to heat the water, she asked, "Are you still working with Pfarrer Bernau?"

"Yes," Ursula said, sighing. "It is tiring on top of my usual work at the prison, but I can't stop now. There are so many people who need to leave this country to stay safe."

"Aren't you afraid?" Anna asked.

Ursula looked at her with big eyes, before she giggled. "Afraid? Of course! There's not a single minute in the day that I'm not frightened. Every time I hear steps behind me, I'm certain it's the Gestapo coming to arrest me."

"But...how can you live like that? Don't you want to stop? And feel safe again?" Anna insisted. Her older sister had never been particularly courageous. She had been *the good girl*, while Anna herself had been the rebellious one, the one who wanted more from life than being a wife and mother.

"I want to stop at least ten times a day," Ursula said as she put a few peppermint leaves into a cup and poured hot water on top. "But then...these people need me. If we can't get them out of the country, sooner or later they will be found and sent to the camps."

Anna sighed. Why was everyone else so much braver than her?

"Enough about me; how's your work?" Ursula asked.

"I've been promoted to team leader of the research group."

"That's a good thing, right?" Ursula asked.

Anna shook her head, tears filling her eyes. "No. Ursula,

you wouldn't believe…they are testing my vaccines on real people."

"What?"

"They've been using mentally ill children…"

"That's disgusting." Ursula put a hand on her hips and stared at her sister with a piercing glance. "You have to stop working there. Today. How can you be a part of that?"

"It's not that easy. I'm not directly involved, and if I don't prepare the bacterial cultures somebody else will. And sometimes sacrifices have to be made for the greater good."

"That's bull. You don't actually believe that baloney, do you?" Ursula's eyes shot daggers at her, but then her glance softened and she patted Anna's arm. "Don't make a pact with the devil, Anna. Walk away."

Anna gave a bitter laugh. "I already sold my body to the devil, remember?"

"I do. Don't sell your soul as well. The Nazis can take everything from you, your possessions, your dignity, your physical integrity, but the one thing they can't take away is your soul. Your ability to make the right choice." After her speech, Ursula suddenly looked tired.

"I should go," Anna murmured. She hadn't come here to be lectured and scolded like a three-year-old. She came because she needed empathy and some sisterly support.

"Don't." Ursula stopped her. "It's time for you to stop putting your ambitions above everything and everyone else. You may be living your dream and climbing the ladder of success, but it's built on the corpses of men, women, and children. Not on your accomplishments."

"Who are you to criticize my choices? You can't even tell Mutter the truth!" Anna yelled at her sister.

"Tell me what?" Mutter asked, coming to stand beside the table. She glared from one daughter to the other, her stare demanding an answer.

Ursula flashed Anna a nasty look and then said what she should have confessed months earlier, "I'm pregnant."

Mutter's face turned ashen and she flopped onto the chair. "You're what?"

"Pregnant," Ursula repeated, shaking with tension.

"How...how could you do something so...so...disgraceful? Haven't I raised you to be a modest girl? One that doesn't..." Mutter closed her eyes, disgust showing in her face. "You can be glad your father isn't home."

None of this would have happened in the first place if he were home, instead of having to go to war. Anna bit her tongue; it was wiser to keep out of the line of fire.

Mutter seemed to recover from the shock, some of the lost color returning to her face. She ran a hand over her hair, smoothing the first streaks of gray, and asked in a much calmer voice, "Who is the...father?"

Ursula begged Anna with her eyes to stay silent, and then confronted her mother, saying, "I can't tell you."

"Why not? Is it so terrible?" Mutter's eyes turned wide as saucers. "It is, isn't it? The father is one of those visitors you've been hiding in the allotment gardens?"

Ursula remained quiet, refusing to answer her mother. Anna, for once, was in full agreement with keeping the parentage of Ursula's baby a secret. The reality was much worse than Mutter imagined. The father wasn't a Jew, but the enemy; one of the hated English bomber pilots bringing death and destruction to the German people.

"I have to leave," Anna announced into the tense quiet. "I'll visit another day."

CHAPTER 23

A nna left the apartment, angry at Ursula, at Mutter, and at Peter. But most of all she was angry with herself. Ursula's pep talk had struck a chord. Was Anna barking up the wrong tree? Was the career she'd worked so hard to obtain worth nothing?

Anna increased her pace, walking all the way to her place at the Charité. She reached the staff building covered in sweat, her heart pounding from the exercise. Did anyone not actively opposing the wrongdoings automatically become a criminal by association? What had happened to the comfortable position inside the silent majority, where people were neither saints nor devils?

Am I a Nazi by definition now? Who can I talk to who won't be judgmental? I need a voice of reason.

She turned on her heel and rushed across the huge compound of the Charité, glancing at the residual damage remaining from the awful destruction inflicted by the recent bombing raid.

Peter will listen without jumping to conclusions. Anna gritted her teeth. He was the last person she wanted to see right now. Not because he'd turned out to be a spy, because truth be told, she longed for Hitler to lose the war and disappear for good. But because she was still livid over the fact that she'd had to find out his secret by accident. A part of her understood why Peter had kept silent, but that didn't lessen the hurt she felt over his lack of faith in her.

Her feet propelled her forward, and for a fleeting moment she considered keeping on running. But where to? What would she do? The crazy idea to volunteer to become a nurse following the front line popped into her head. But just thinking about giving up her position at the Charité made her heart ache. She loved her work, despite everything.

I'm not cut out to be a hero. I'm a failure.

Anna reached the end of the hospital grounds, and the inner turmoil brought on by her self-recriminations had left her in a frantic haze, unable to form a clear thought. As she turned the corner, a church bell chimed twelve times, and reminded her of her sister Lotte. And Ursula. And Pfarrer Bernau. She'd met him a few times when planning Lotte's escape. He wouldn't judge. He might even help her to gain clarity.

With newfound hope, Anna turned back and walked the forty-five minutes until she reached his parish. She found him sitting on a pew at the front of the church and quietly took a seat next to him. He looked at her and then asked, "What can I do for you, my child?"

"Father, I feel like such a failure," she started, trying hard to keep the swelling tears from her eyes.

"Aren't you Ursula's sister? Anna Klausen?" He scrutinized her with his warm brown eyes.

"Yes, but…" She nodded and then the words burst out of her, revealing everything that aggrieved her. "You see, everyone is doing something. But I'm a failure."

"My child, there are many forms of resistance, and not everyone is cut out to be a hero."

"But how come both of my sisters can be heroes, and I cannot?"

"This is where you are wrong," Pfarrer Bernau said, smiling at her. "You have done a courageous thing in Ravensbrück."

"But what should I do now?" Anna couldn't hold back her tears.

"Look, God loves all his children, and he has given each of us different talents and abilities for a reason." He handed her a handkerchief. "We each have an internal moral compass that we use to guide our decisions in this life. That compass is developed from the time we are small children and is rooted in our belief system. It is part of who we are, and when we try to go against it, we suffer. The important thing is to stay true to yourself despite the circumstances. Each of us has to look deep inside and find out what we really want."

"I always thought I knew what I wanted, but I'm not so sure anymore…" she pressed out between sniffs.

"This is a question only you can answer." He must have seen the despair in her eyes, because he folded his hands in his lap and added, "I do have one piece of advice for you – listen to your heart. Do what your heart tells you is morally right, whether it is the popular or safe thing to do or not. A person who can sleep at peace with himself, even behind bars, is happier than the person who is afraid to shut their eyes because they fear facing the nightmares caused by their own actions."

The priest's words caused peace to settle in Anna's heart. "Thank you, Father, you've given me much to think about."

"Go in peace. You'll do the right thing, I'm sure of it." He smiled and blessed her by making the sign of the cross on her forehead.

Anna spent the rest of the day thinking – and avoiding Peter. She didn't need the additional strain to deal with her confusing emotions towards him.

When Professor Scherer stopped by her office the next morning, she knew exactly what she wanted. She'd spent the better part of the weekend rehearsing her words, and only hoped she could get it all out before losing her courage.

"Good morning, Professor Scherer," she greeted him.

"Good morning, Fräulein Klausen. You definitely made an impression at the Minister's gathering."

"Thank you." She hesitated for a moment, unsure how to tackle the enormous weight pressing on her soul.

"I see you have already planned the direction the next round of experiments should take," he said to her, scanning the scribbled notes on her notepad.

"About that…Professor Scherer…I am not comfortable doing experiments on live humans. Not until we have narrowed down what we think is a viable vaccine in the laboratory studies."

"Fräulein Klausen…" The professor paused as if he was at a loss for words. He scratched his head and then looked at her, taking inventory of her. "That is unexpected."

"I realize that's not what you were expecting to hear, but it is how I feel," she said, slowly building up the confidence to stand her ground.

"You are being overly sensitive." He looked at her with sad puppy eyes, and in that moment, she wanted to slap the condescending expression from his face. "I'm afraid Professor Knaus was right, and I'm placing too much confidence in a woman. I thought you were of a different stamp. I truly thought you had the drive and ambition to become a successful scientist."

"I do. I work harder than anyone else to succeed, but knowing people will be suffering because of my endeavors? That doesn't sit well with me."

The professor shook his head. "Not people. Sub-humans or prisoners, remember that."

"They still feel pain and fear," Anna argued, knowing she'd already lost the battle.

"Some things have to be done, whether you like them or not. Our work bids fair to save hundreds of thousands of upstanding members of society. Right now, the Eastern Front is breaking down, our military is retreating, and our research is needed now more than ever. Think of all the valiant soldiers protecting our frontiers from the evil Red Army. Don't you think that a few suffering retards are worth it when we can enable thousands to return to embrace their wives and kiss their children?"

A shiver ran down Anna's spine. Did the *Greater Good* really justify continuing to take actions that went against her values? And who got to decide which sacrifice was worth it? Who decided what was good and what was evil? She recalled Pfarrer Bernau's words that each person had to decide for themselves. Anna was lost in her thoughts for so long, Professor Scherer took her silence as a sign that she wasn't going to relent in her stance.

"Fräulein Klausen, you do realize that if you refuse to run these experiments you will lose your job? I've pulled many strings to push you forward in your career, had to battle the resistance from more conservative colleagues who thought a woman had no place in science." He glanced at her and then used his last ace, saying, "I know you may have reservations about going forward with these experiments, but it's time to put aside your personal feelings and act in the best interest of our Fatherland. And don't forget your friend Alexandra who wants to become a *Wehrmacht-shelferin* and for whom you asked me to write a recommendation." The threat lingered in the air.

The icy hand of desperation grabbed her heart and threatened to crush it. Yesterday everything had seemed so easy. But today? Was fighting over a dozen mental cases worth ruining her career, and Lotte's too? Wouldn't she do more bad than good by impeding her sister from *helping the war effort* by possibly shortening the war and saving millions of lives on both sides? Her head spun until it ached.

With her, or without her, the experiments would be performed. Professor Scherer would simply find a less scrupulous person to take her place.

Anna took a steadying breath and then blinked several

times. "Forgive me, Professor Scherer. Of course I will not refuse your wishes."

He relaxed and smiled saying, "That's quite alright, my dear. Let's put this behind us and move forward, shall we?"

Anna nodded, her stomach in knots even as she did so. "Yes. I'll give more thought to the experiments today."

"Grand. I'll stop by tomorrow to hear your thoughts."

Anna watched him leave, and slumped on her chair, self-hatred churning in her stomach.

CHAPTER 24

After an exhausting day at work, Anna returned home, her entire being aching with guilt and shame. It was so wrong, and yet, Professor Scherer had once again convinced her to walk down that slippery path.

Emotionally drained and exhausted, all she wanted to do was sleep. And forget. But when she approached the apartment building, a huge man sat on the steps, jumping up when he saw her approach.

"Anna...please. Can we talk?" Peter begged her. "Please?"

She squinted her eyes at him, nodding. She was too tired to fight another battle today. Then she walked around him, needing her space, because she knew the moment he touched her she would sink bawling into his arms.

"Come in," she said as she unlocked the door and set down her purse on the side table. Biting her lower lip, she turned to look at him. "What did you want to talk about?"

"Anna, can we sit down, please?" Peter held out his hand

and waited until she joined him on the couch. "I'm so sorry you had to find out like this. Will you let me explain?"

She nodded but didn't look at him. Peter sighed as if he expected as much and then began to talk.

"I was born in Poland."

"You already said that," she commented quietly.

"Both of my parents were healers, much to the dismay of my grandparents who had hoped my father would one day run their farm on the outskirts of the town. My siblings and I grew up speaking both Polish and German. At that time, it was normal for children of Polish intellectuals to learn several languages. I also speak decent English and Russian. But I digress. When Hitler invaded, I was an officer in the Polish army. After the devastating defeat, my unit fled via Romania and Iran to Britain."

"You did?" Anna couldn't help but look at him. Fleeing thousands of miles across Europe seemed an impossible undertaking.

"It's not something I'm especially proud of," he said, nervously twisting hands. "But at that time it was the best thing to do. We wouldn't be of much use for Poland in a prisoner-of-war camp...or as forced laborers in the Reich." He gave a bitter laugh. "Many of my men died, but a majority reached Britain. Some joined the British Army, others decided to be repatriated and joined the Polish resistance, the Armia Krajowa or Home Army as you would call it."

"And you? How did you end up here?" Anna asked despite her intention to remain silent.

"Me?" A soft smile quirked his lips and he took her hand. "At first I joined the British Army and asked to be put to service. I was part of the British Expeditionary Force in France – you know how well that worked out." He rubbed his hand across his beard before he continued, "My men and I got evacuated from Dunkirk."

"Oh," was all Anna could say. She'd never understood why Hitler had allowed the English to evacuate their soldiers. Rumors had it that he'd wanted to show his good-will and convince them to join forces with him. But those times had long passed...

"It was godawful. When I returned to England, the SOE recruited me to work for them and arranged for me to come into Germany."

Without noticing it, Anna had inched closer to Peter, staring at his lips, soaking up every word he spoke. "That's how you came to work for Professor Scherer?"

He reached out an arm and tucked her in by his side. "Someone on the inside made a suggestion, and since they had gained the trust of those in power, their suggestion was taken without question. It was the perfect position to have. The professor is socially active and as you've seen, the men pulling the strings of the war value his opinions so much, they openly discuss matters in his presence. As his security guard and driver, I attract no suspicion and can overhear these conversations."

"Does the professor know?" Anna asked.

"No. He may not be a Nazi by conviction, but he would never go against them. He knows that would be the end of his career, and he values his status too much."

A pang of guilt hit Anna's stomach. *Same here.*

Peter took her face into his hands and pressed a sweet

kiss on her lips. "Can you forgive me for pulling the wool over your eyes?"

"Perhaps," she said. He didn't have to know that she'd already forgiven him. Trust was a tricky issue, and she would have done the same thing in his shoes.

"Sweetest Anna, believe me, I wanted to tell you so many times, but...you seemed so enthralled with the glamor and adulation of the Nazis, I wasn't sure where your loyalties actually lay."

Anna laughed sharply saying, "That's because we don't know much about each other."

"I would like to change that. Can you forgive me and give me a second chance?" Peter pressed another kiss on her cheek, and Anna's mind went blissfully blank. She grabbed his shoulders like a drowning woman, and soaked up his calming presence.

"If you promise to keep no more secrets," she answered.

"Promise." He grinned and took her mouth in a passionate kiss. Anna felt as if she were floating on cloud nine, and soon enough he scooped her up into his arms and carried her over to the bedroom. She leaned her head against his broad chest, and giggled as he settled her carefully on the bed.

"Wait!" She shot up and searched his face as if seeing him for the first time.

"What is it, sweetheart?"

"I don't even know your real name! How can I do this if I don't even know who you are?" Anna whispered.

"I'm the man who loves you. That's who I am." Peter chuckled. "My real name is Piotr Zdanek. I am a member of the Polish Army, a member of the British Army, and currently acting as a spy for both."

Anna slung her arms around his neck and pushed back so hard he lost his balance and toppled on top of her. When he placed little kisses down her neck and her collarbone, she moaned with delight. But the moment he pushed his hands beneath her blouse, she sucked in a breath and clenched her hands by her sides as the old fears tried to surface.

"Are you afraid of me?" Peter, sensing her sudden tension, stopped kissing his way across her jawline and looked deep into her eyes.

"Not of you, but I am afraid," Anna whispered. She knew she should tell him the secret she'd been hiding, but she wasn't that brave.

"Do you want me to stop? We can wait," Peter said.

"No. I have waited so long. I want to stop being afraid. Please help me."

Peter kissed her again and then unbuttoned her blouse. "Are you sure about this?"

Anna nodded, seeking the love in his eyes. "I'm positive. Show me that being with you is as wonderful as I've imagined."

CHAPTER 25

Anna and Peter emerged from the bedroom to scour her kitchen for food. While Anna fixed them something to eat, Peter set the table and asked about her day at work.

"Exhausting," she answered, not keen on delving deeper into the topic.

"Professor Scherer seemed concerned about you today. What happened?" Of course Peter had noticed she was trying to evade the topic.

"You remember what I told you about the medical experiments?" Anna said, unable to face Peter.

"I do," he said with a low voice.

Anna stirred the soup with increased violence, saying, "He has put me in charge. I am supposed to devise the new experiments that will be carried out using not only the children, but also prisoners at nearby camps." She stopped stirring and turned around, shooting daggers at him as if he were the evil person in the situation. "He doesn't care how much these people suffer or how many die in the process!"

"But you do?" Peter said.

"How can I not? The children may be retarded, but they are still human and feel pain…how can I be the instrument of their torture and death?"

"You discussed your concerns with Professor Scherer?" Peter stood and closed the distance between them.

Anna nodded and then changed it to a shrug saying, "Kind of. I told him I wasn't comfortable using the vaccines until we had more evidence that they work. He said only a woman could be so weak. And then he threatened my job and the recommendation for my sis…friend if I didn't obey his orders."

"What did you do?" Peter wrapped his arms around her.

"I agreed. What else was I to do? But I don't know if I can go through with it," she said, leaning into him and taking the pot from the stove. "Our soup is ready."

"Anna, one thing I've learned throughout this war…there is always a third option. It might not be visible right now, but it's there. You have to look for it."

"Do you really believe this?" Anna asked, a glimmer of hope breaking through the darkness that enveloped her life.

"I know for sure. Look for it…it's there. And now let's eat. I'm starving."

"Who isn't these days?" she answered and poured the majority of the soup into his bowl.

"I love you, sweetheart. No more secrets," he said, wolfing down the meal. Anna blushed and focused on her spoon. But trust went both ways, right?

"There's something else I have to tell you," she said and put down her spoon with a clinking sound

"More bad news?" He glanced at her with worry.

"No, just more secrets." Anna gathered her courage and told him about her *dead* sister Lotte, who was well, alive, and lived now under the name of Alexandra, needing the professor's recommendation for her radio assistant training and her plan to work as a spy.

Peter laughed. "Looks like your sister and I will soon be colleagues. I would love to meet her one day."

Once they finished their meal, Anna asked him to stay overnight and soon she slept in the secure embrace of his arms.

The next morning after kissing Peter goodbye, she loped to the laboratories. Anna could sense something was amiss, but she didn't recognize it on first sight.

But as she entered the lecture hall she saw workers systematically disassembling the secretarial offices. Metal desks, chairs, and even office equipment encased in metal were being removed and loaded into trucks.

She hurried to the laboratory, where she found a colleague standing in the doorway, watching with a long face, and she asked him, "What's going on?"

"The order came in this morning that all things made of metal have to be turned over to the war effort. There's not enough metal to continue making tanks and weapons."

"They're taking everything metal, even from hospitals?" Anna asked, incredulous.

"No, hospitals are exempt. But this building is only clerical, so it has to comply." The colleague left to try and salvage at least the metals they needed for their research work.

Anna looked after him, thinking about how everyone would have to find materials to substitute for the metal they were turning over. *Substitutes! There's always a third option. Thank you, Peter.*

She yelped with joy and rushed off to set her plan in motion. After taking a walk down to the storeroom to grab several IV bags of saline solution, she diligently prepared the syringes for today's experiments.

When Professor Scherer dropped by to discuss the progress, she showed him her notes and her plans on how to complement the lab experiments with tests on humans, and handed him the syringes with a smile. She had no idea how long she could get away with giving the test patients nothing but saline water injections before she was found out, but it would buy her time to find another solution.

CHAPTER 26

P rofessor Scherer received the *Kriegsverdienstkreuz* for his outstanding merits in the war effort. The Cross of Merit was the highest award a civilian could receive. To honor the work of his research team, he invited the entire staff to a small celebration in the auditorium.

Anna sneaked into the room after everyone else, because she'd wanted to finish her calculations. Professor Scherer had almost finished his acceptance speech, thanking everyone on the team.

"...will assume the professorship in internal medicine by the end of this month. Please welcome him to our team." The position had been vacant for a few months and as far as Anna knew there had been a number of applicants.

She weaved her way through the crowd to congratulate Professor Scherer, and give the new professor a warm welcome. But she froze in her tracks, and felt the blood drain from her face when she recognized the man standing beside Professor Scherer.

Professor Scherer noticed her before she could slip back into the crowd and motioned her forward saying, "Doctor Tretter, you remember Fräulein Klausen? She's my head of bacterial research, and may I say she's one of the best students I've ever had."

"Nurse Anna. It's a pleasure to see you again." Doctor Tretter shook her hand with a repugnant smile.

Anna's knees became soft as jelly, and the bile rose in her throat as she stared at his hand grasping hers. The image of sticking a knife deep into his hand brought some relief, and she found the strength to breathe again. She withdrew her hand and turned towards the professor saying, "Congratulations for being awarded the Cross of Merit."

"Thank you, Fräulein Klausen, but I could not have had this success without my team."

She smiled and stepped aside to let others congratulate him. But Doctor Tretter wouldn't let her go that easily. He followed her and grabbed her arm, leering at her. "It's been a while. I've missed the fun we had together. I look forward to catching up."

Anna curled her hands into fists, fear moving like molasses through her veins, as the memories of his past torment assailed her. She shook her head and backed away, her eyes wide with terror and her heart missing a beat or two.

When she hit the wall, she put a hand out to ward him off. "St...stay...away from...me."

"Oh, I don't see that happening. Do you? You haven't forgotten that it takes only one word from me to have you executed?"

Anna couldn't move. Panic held her rigid with an iron grip and paralyzed her body. When she didn't answer, he continued, "Perhaps you should give me a tour of the facility. I'm sure we can find an unused room for a few minutes."

She blinked, hoping he'd disappear. But this wasn't one of her harrowing nightmares; it was T the devil in the flesh. Anna knew without a shadow of doubt if she gave into his demands today, he would control her forever. She wouldn't survive if he raped her again. No, she couldn't allow that to happen.

"Anna, here you are," Peter said, appearing out of nowhere, registering the situation with a single glance. "I need to talk to you." Then he sent a menacing stare at Doctor Tretter, who showed no intention of letting her go. "Please excuse us."

Anna ducked around Doctor Tretter, ignoring his threatening glance, and made straight for Peter, who ushered her into the hallway grinding his jaw. "What was that all about? Are you alright?"

"I am now, thanks to you." Anna sent him a small smile. This wasn't the place or time to reveal her secret, so she said, "Walk me back to my laboratory?"

"You're not staying for the celebration?" Peter asked.

Anna shook her head. "I already congratulated the professor and I have several experiments going that need my attention now."

"I'll walk you over." He took her hand and they walked in silence, the ghost of Doctor Tretter hovering between them. Anna knew she should tell Peter, but right now she was too agitated to hold a conversation.

She leaned against Peter and kissed him. "You should get back to the celebration, or the professor will be wondering about your whereabouts."

"I'd rather stay…"

"Peter, we both have our work to do and I can take care of myself," she said, although she wasn't sure if she could. Not if T the devil showed up again.

"I'll kill him if he ever touches you again," Peter growled, and by the look in his eyes she knew it wasn't an empty threat.

"He won't." Anna exuded a confidence she didn't have, and turned to walk into the vacant laboratory with a queasy feeling in her stomach. But she couldn't let Peter get involved in this. His situation was dangerous enough as it was; he didn't need the added risk of dealing with someone as perfidious as Doctor Tretter.

A half an hour later her hopes were dashed when Doctor Tretter walked into her laboratory space. Since he didn't shut the door, Anna was sure he merely wanted to intimidate and scare her into compliance. But that didn't make him less harrowing.

"What do you want?" she asked with all the strength she could muster, grateful for the laboratory table full of glass and potentially dangerous solutions physically separating them.

He smirked and lowered his voice to a menacing growl: "I wanted to make sure you knew that I won't have you sleeping with another man. If you have any thoughts of giving that lousy scum what is mine, I promise you will both regret your betrayal." Then he turned on his heel and left.

Anna clasped the edge of the table to prevent her knees from buckling. She'd been afraid before, but now, she was petrified. By the time Anna finished her tasks, she had worked herself into a full-blown panic.

Afraid to be alone, she went straight to Peter's place. He greeted her with a huge smile, but after one glance at her face, he pulled her into his arms and carried her to the armchair, where he held her until she stopped shaking.

After a long while, Peter spoke, "Sweetheart, it breaks my heart to see you terrified like this. Please let me help. Tell me what's going on."

She nodded and hid her face against his chest, inhaling his unique scent, gathering the courage to come clean. "That man…he was the head physician in Ravensbrück. He's a horrible man – no, man is too kind a word. He's a monster. The things he's done…"

"Shush. He can't hurt you here." Peter stroked his hand across her hair like her mother had done when she was a little child.

"But he can. He's threatened to have me executed if I don't do what he wants." Anna broke out in sobs, wetting his shirt with her tears.

"I must have missed something. Start from the beginning. Why does this man think he can have you executed? What is it he thinks you've done?"

"He knows I've done it. He was there." She took a deep breath and then told him the details of the story how Ursula and she had rescued their sister Lotte.

"Clever girl," Peter murmured in approval and then he asked the question Anna dreaded to answer, "What did he want?"

Her entire body tensed and trembled as memories of that day came rushing back, and she couldn't form a word if her life depended on it. Peter muttered a few Polish curses and rubbed his hands up and down her back in a soothing gesture. "Don't answer that. I get the picture. He's the one who raped you?"

"How did you know?" Anna whispered, afraid to look at him.

"I'm not stupid, Anna. I could tell that someone had abused you, but I didn't want to add to your distress by asking questions. I figured you would talk about it when you were ready."

New tears flooded her face and she threw herself into his arms. Peter simply held her while she cried. For herself. For Lotte. For his other victims, the *Króliki*, human guinea pigs, at Ravensbrück who'd had to endure the most excruciating medical experiments at his hands. When she had no more tears to cry, she lay against Peter's chest, his shirt soaked with her tears, and said, "He's promised to continue where he left off."

"Over my dead body," Peter growled, squeezing her fiercely against his chest.

"But...but...what can I do? What can you do?"

"For now, nothing. But trust me, I'll cut off not only his hands should he ever reach out to touch you again."

"You can't do that!" Anna pushed away from him to look into his scornful blue eyes. "The Gestapo would happily make minced meat out of you. There's no way I'm going to allow you to do this for me!"

Peter chuckled and pressed a kiss on her cheek. "That's

why I love you so much, because you're such an undaunted young lady."

"Peter, I'm serious..."

"And I'm serious too. What kind of man would I be if I didn't protect the woman I love?"

CHAPTER 27

The next day Anna paid a visit to Mutter and Ursula. She caught one of the infrequent busses, and crossed the devastated city. Since she lived in the staff housing, she rarely left the Charité grounds and had forgotten how god-awful the situation in Berlin was.

At long last the incessant air raids had stopped, as if the Allies had decided there was nothing left worth bombing in the capital. According to the radio, the Allies were now focusing their air raids over France. Speculation had it the Allies were planning an invasion somewhere on the French Atlantic coast. Damaging infrastructure was their preparation for crippling the German defenses.

Anna had never spent much time thinking about what would happen when the war ended. Despite the constant rallying to persist, most of her colleagues doubted that Germany would win this war. Not after the Americans poured millions and millions of dollars, material, and soldiers into this craziness. And even the Russians, who had been one step from defeat when Hitler's army stormed Moscow in the fall of 1941, had recovered and regrouped and were now annihilating division after division of the German Wehrmacht.

Most everyone wanted the war to end, but looking at the devastation the bus passed, it dawned on Anna that it wouldn't be the magical return to glory that everyone expected. Not for a long time. The winners would be so full of hatred and repulsion for the German people – more so when they found out about the things happening in the camps – that Anna feared they might kill all of them, like they had razed the cities and towns across Germany.

Raw with emotion she trudged up the stairs to Mutter's apartment. Mid-flight, she met her neighbor walking downwards.

"Frau Weber, how are you today?" Anna plastered on a polite smile.

"I'm fine. But I'm worried about your sister Ursula." Frau Weber blocked the stairs, obviously on the hunt for gossip.

Anna feigned ignorance, saying, "I'm sure she's fine."

"Well, there's something going on. She rarely leaves the apartment these days. Is she still grieving about Lotte's death? Poor girl. So young. But also with a tongue that couldn't be tamed. Your mother never explained what happened." Frau Weber gave her a curious look.

"She contracted typhus and couldn't be saved," Anna said, hoping this would be enough to get Frau Weber out of her hair.

"Poor girl...it's been, how long? Three months? And

there still hasn't been a memorial service for her. And where's her grave?"

You stupid snitcher. There won't be a memorial service because she isn't really dead. Anna tried her best to make a sad face. "Yes, it's such a tragedy. We never received her body. Quarantine restrictions, you know? The authorities were afraid the corpse might spread the disease to our family and even to our neighbors." Anna had to bite on her cheeks to prevent herself from laughing at Frau Weber's horrified face.

"Oh," the woman said and backed away from Anna.

"The authorities were right," Anna added with a devilish joy, and then continued, "I care for patients with typhus, tuberculosis, dysentery, and cholera on a daily basis and I know how easy it is to contract such a deadly disease." She took a step towards her harping neighbor.

"I...I am in a hurry," Frau Weber said and fled down the stairs.

Anna grinned and knocked on the door. Not having to put up with Frau Weber was a definite advantage of having moved out. She remembered all too well the time Frau Weber had called the Gestapo on them while they were hiding the British pilot – the father of Ursula's baby.

"Anna, darling, how are you?" Mutter asked as she opened the door.

"I'm fine." Anna entered the apartment and left her coat on the rack, noticing three coats already hanging on the hooks. "You're having guests?"

"So I wish," Mutter said with a tired sigh. "The housing office has assigned a bombed-out person to live with us.

164

Sabine is staying in your room and Ursula has moved her things into my room. We were lucky they didn't assign us another person to take up quarters in the living room."

"Is she here?" Anna glanced around and then followed her mother into the kitchen.

"No, she's working at the ammunition factory." Mutter heated water for tea. "Sabine is Ursula's age and thankfully she's a tidy person. Her husband is dead, and given the decay of moral standards amongst your generation," Mutter said, pausing only long enough to give a pointed look at Ursula, who shoved her big belly into the room, "I have told her that no men are allowed in this house under any circumstances."

"Hello, sister." Anna ignored her mother's comment and hugged Ursula. "How are you?"

"Much better since I went to the ration office and registered my pregnancy. You won't believe the kind of extra food we're getting now," Ursula said.

"You need it." Anna flopped onto the chair and took the cup of steaming tea Mutter handed her.

"Maybe you can talk some sense into your sister," Mutter said to Anna.

"What's she talking about?"

"Mutter thinks I should go to the country. To Aunt Lydia's," Ursula answered as she received a cup of tea as well.

"It's not the worst idea I've heard of," Anna said slowly.

"I don't want to leave Berlin. Pfarrer Bernau needs my help. Now more than ever." Ursula grimaced at them.

Mutter shook her head, saying, "You have a baby to

think about now. This...work you're doing is endangering both of you. With my sister you'll be safe, get better food and more sleep."

Anna could see a fight brewing and changed the subject. "Have you heard from Richard again?"

Mutter sent her a scowl. "Richard! Don't even get me started on your brother! That reckless boy has sent me a letter that he requested a return to combat in lieu of staying wherever he was safely tucked behind a desk. Can you believe this?"

Anna couldn't. Richard had always been the bookworm of the family, a shy, quiet, and thin boy, who was happy to leave the limelight to his three sisters. One year older than wildcat Lotte, people had often mentioned that she behaved more like a boy than he did. It was beyond Anna's comprehension that even her withdrawn brother suddenly showed heroic qualities while she still peed in her pants over Doctor Tretter's threats.

"Mutter, you don't know what kind of things he had to do at his desk job," Ursula said, putting a calming hand on her mother's arm and sending Anna a glance that said *I'll bet he prefers dying on the battlefield to being responsible for some of the things we know are happening.*

"When will this war end?" Mutter asked the rhetorical question with a desolate tone in her voice.

"Hopefully soon," Anna answered and then added, "Lotte called me a while ago to remind me of the fact that she has turned eighteen."

"My little one. I hope the nuns can instill some obedience in her," Muter said.

"She's not in the convent anymore," Anna blurted out and then clasped a hand in front of her mouth.

"What do you mean? Where is she?" Mutter squinted her eyes at Anna, who blushed furiously as she realized her mistake.

"I don't know, but she called me because she needed a letter of reference. To be accepted as *Wehrmachtshelferin* and start radio operator training," Anna murmured.

Mutter's face became ashen and for long moments one could have heard a pin drop.

"A radio operator? What is that girl thinking?" Mutter finally asked.

"That's a hell of a dangerous position–" Ursula said, interrupted by the tsking sound her mother made at the use of this inappropriate word.

"I'm sorry, Mutter, but radio operators follow the front line to report back to headquarters. Since it is so dangerous, they've been desperately looking for volunteers," Ursula explained.

Mutter closed her eyes and said, "I don't know what's come over my children lately. Nobody heeds my advice anymore."

Much later, Ursula accompanied her sister to the bus station and used the time alone with her to ask, "What made Lotte change her mind and work for the Nazis?"

"Not for the Nazis, against them. She's put her mind to working for the Allies as a spy." Anna hugged her sister tight, seeing that her bus was nearing the stop.

"Jesus. She'll get caught and then? She'll wish herself back in Ravensbrück." A shudder racked Ursula's body. "I've seen what the Gestapo does with their prisoners. The ones who arrive at our prison seldom look like human beings anymore."

"We have to trust that she won't get caught. We both know that short of shackling her to a pole, there's not much to keep her from pursuing her plan," Anna said, taking a step back from Ursula and hopping on the bus. "Take care!"

CHAPTER 28

Anna went straight to Peter's place and knocked. After she'd surprised him transmitting the radio message, he always double-checked that he'd locked the door

"Hello, sweetheart." He greeted her with a kiss and then locked the door behind her. "How was the visit with your family?"

"Nice, but..." Anna bent down to take off her shoes. "The housing office assigned them a bombed-out victim. And Mutter wants Ursula to live in the country with my aunt until the baby has arrived."

"That's not a bad idea, actually." Peter grinned and whirled her around. "I'll take you out to the motion pictures after dinner, but first I need to transmit a message."

"You do whatever you need to do and I'll cook. Mutter gave me a chunk of sausage that Aunt Lydia sent. And now let me down." Anna laughed and jiggled her legs in the air.

"I will not," Peter protested, and carried her all the way

to the small kitchenette before he set her down and stole another kiss.

Anna hummed a melody to a tune on the radio as she prepared the feast. The familiar tapping coming from the bedroom was drowned out when she started chopping cabbage, carrots, and potatoes to make a casserole for them.

"Hmm, that smells good. What is it?"

She spun around at the sound of the voice and gasped in shock, saying, "What are you doing here?"

"I followed you," Doctor Tretter answered with a leer.

"How did you get in?" She was positive Peter had locked the door behind her after entering.

He proudly held up a key. Anna wanted to slap it out of his arrogant hand. "This is the master key to all the staff apartments in the Charité compound. I happened to come into possession of it."

"You need to leave. I didn't invite you here." Anna glanced at the kitchen knife she held in her hand and clasped it tighter. She couldn't yell for Peter's help because he was transmitting a message to London. If T the devil caught a glimpse of the radio equipment, neither her life nor Peter's was worth a single *Pfennig* anymore.

"Where are your manners, Nurse Anna?" He looked around the apartment. "So, this is where you live. Nice." Then his glance fell on Peter's hat and driver's uniform hanging from one of the hooks beside the door.

He turned towards her, fire and anger churning in his eyes. "Whore! I warned you what would happen if you betrayed me!"

"I may have been a whore for you, but not anymore." Anna felt rage coiling in her blood, pushing the fear aside and giving her a strength she didn't know she possessed. "You leave now and never bother me again, or–"

"Or what? Will you call that lover of yours to come to your aid? Do you really think he'll go up against me? He's nothing but a chauffeur, a servant. Oh no," he spat. He approached her, his eyes glinting with pure evil. "You are mine. To do with whatever I like. However I like. Whenever I like. I own you and you will be my whore for as long as I see fit."

Anna's anger snaked up her torso, and landed on her lips effectively sealing them shut. The radio played the last notes of a popular song, and then silence fell over the apartment; a silence that was only pierced by the muted tapping noises coming from behind the bedroom door.

Doctor Tretter froze. "What is that? Who is in there?"

"Nobody. Get out." Anna knew she had to do something to stop him and stepped into his path.

"Get out of my way," he commanded and pushed her to the side as if she were nothing but a pesky insect. Then he stormed across the room and shoved open the door to find Peter bent over his transmitter.

"You? The Gestapo will delight in my discovery," Doctor Tretter said with a cruel smile, and turned on his heel to pick up the phone. But Anna was faster.

"No you won't. You've done enough damage for a life-time." Then she launched her arm at him and slit his carotid artery with the kitchen knife she still gripped in her hand.

What happened next, she did not remember.

"Anna? Sweetheart? Are you alright?" She heard Peter's voice through the thunderous rushing in her ears. Still unable to properly focus, she saw his shadow moving in front of her and felt him slapping her cheek to return the blood to her head. "Please, say something!"

"I guess...I am...fine." Her mouth was filled with cotton balls, but at least her vision returned and she could now clearly see Peter hovering over her. He must have caught her falling as she fainted and carried her to the bed. "Where is...is he?"

"He's never going to hurt you again." Peter sat down on the bed beside her and gently removed the knife from her fingers.

"I killed him," she whispered, nausea bubbling up the back of her throat. She'd deliberately taken the life of another human being. No matter how despicable the man, she'd murdered him in cold blood. The monstrosity of her actions seeped into her brain, her bones, and her heart. She had killed an important Party member by her own hand.

"Shush, try not to think about it right now. You saved my life, and yours, too." Peter soothed her and wrapped his arms around her shoulders. No matter how tender his ministrations, Anna's body still trembled under the weight of what she had done. "Wait, I'll be right back." He disappeared to the kitchenette and returned moments later with am acrid-smelling transparent liquid in a glass.

"What's that?" Anna whispered, too drained to raise her hands. She wished a fissure would open up in the floorboards to swallow her whole.

"Vodka. Drink this. It helps." He put the glass to her lips and made her drink up.

He was right. The vodka burned down her throat, returning warmth into her shaking limbs and benumbing her brain enough to stop thinking about the blood sputtering from Doctor Tretter's neck. When Peter made to leave her side, she held onto his hand whispering, "Please. Stay."

"For as long as you need me," he said, and held her tight. The alcohol did its job and she relaxed against Peter's chest, and then tears started to flow. The longer he held her, the more she cried. "Cry as much as you need. It helps," Peter said in a soothing voice, stroking his hand up and down her back. And she did. She wept, yelled, and screamed until she was hoarse and there were no more tears to cry.

When she stopped, Peter kissed her and said, "You try to sleep, and I'll take care of...him." He got up, changed into worn and faded clothes, and rolled up his sleeves.

Anna closed her eyes and must have dozed off, because when she woke later, she heard the sound of cabinets opening and running water. Several minutes later Peter returned with a hard expression on his face and said, "Done."

She did not dare to ask what he had done and how he had disposed of the corpse. She simply invited him beneath her blanket and pressed herself against his strong body. Tomorrow she would deal with the consequences of her actions.

CHAPTER 29

The next morning Anna woke up with the feeling that something awful had happened. She sat up and was rubbing the sleep from her eyes, when the memories came rushing back.

I killed a man.

"Peter?" she yelped in a high-pitched voice.

"Good morning, sweetheart." He entered the room with a towel slung around his hips, his full chest hair still damp from the shower he'd just exited. But Anna had no eyes for the perfect body of the man she loved so much.

"I need...we need...what will..." The words tumbled out in the same mishmash as the thoughts whirling in her head.

"Shush." He placed a kiss on her lips, and his presence slowed down the train of her thoughts. "This is what I want you to do. First, you stop by your apartment and freshen up before reporting to work."

"Work? How can I show up at work today? After..." Anna swallowed, but the panic refused to go down.

"You need to act normal. Go through your routines like every other day. Pretend you haven't seen *him* since the day of the celebration in the auditorium."

"Act normal?" she asked, wondering what that even looked like. *I executed a man with my own hands last night. How does a cold-blooded killer behave?*

Peter pulled her from the bed and hugged her for a long moment, saying, "Now get dressed and go. Don't forget to look as impeccable as you always do." Then he swatted her backside to make her move. Her clothes were covered in blood, but Anna put them on, moving like a puppet on strings. So focused was she on her acting-normal charade, she forgot to say goodbye to Peter as she exited his apartment.

Thankfully, it was still early and she didn't encounter a soul on the short walk over to her own place, where she stepped beneath the shower, fully clothed. She scrubbed her clothes and herself, and washed her hair, until all traces of the doctor's blood had gone. But looking around her, she saw red spots everywhere. She knew it was an illusion, her tortured mind playing tricks on her, because there couldn't be blood in her apartment. Or on her hands…

Plastering a smile on her face, she left her place and reported to work. Nothing happened and nobody seemed to miss Doctor Tretter. By the time she went to the canteen for lunch, she had relaxed a bit and even managed to laugh at the silly jokes of one of her colleagues.

Then Professor Scherer asked all the team leaders to meet in his office with two men in civilian suits flanking him, Anna's heart stopped beating.

"Ladies and gentlemen, there may have been a crime at

the Charité," the professor said in a shaken voice. He raised a tapered finger, and pointed at the two men in gray. "These gentlemen are from the Gestapo, and need to question every single one of you and your team members about the disappearance of Doctor Tretter."

A murmur went through the room, and Anna's palms became damp with cold sweat.

They're going to see right through me. They're going to torture me, and force me to confess. They're going to execute me.

They know I killed him.

"But, Professor Scherer, wasn't the new professor due to arrive two weeks from now?" one of the older doctors asked.

"Unfortunately..." One of the Gestapo officers took a step forward, and pierced one after another of the dozen people in the room with his steel-blue eyes. The murmuring faded away, and Anna was sure she wasn't the only one on pins and needles. The Gestapo had the ability to chill even the most innocent child to the bone, making him rack his brain trying to remember what he might have done wrong.

Strangely enough, this knowledge filled Anna with confidence. In her childhood, she had honed the skill of making anyone believe in her innocence. Play-acting that had worked on her mother would work on the Gestapo lads as well. It must. Or she'd be executed and tossed aside as if she'd meant nothing. Along with Peter. And God knows who else.

"...Doctor Tretter arrived at the Charité last night. He parked his automobile in the lot, and picked up a key to his assigned apartment from the security guards. Since then he hasn't been seen," the Gestapo officer said, letting his eyes rake over the gathered crowd, no doubt seeking for telltale body language.

Anna channeled her best acting skills, and slipped into the role of Fräulein Klausen, the head of bacterial research who only lived for her work, relaxing the tension from her muscles, but adopting a sorrowful expression. Anna, the cold-blooded killer, remained temporarily locked deep down along with her memories of the pivotal moment where her life went off the rails.

One by one, the team leaders and later on the team members were led into a room and questioned by the two Gestapo officers.

"Did Doctor Tretter contact you last night?" the man with the steel-blue eyes asked.

"No, Officer."

"Why not?" the other one said.

Anna blinked in confusion. *That's part of their game.* "He had no reason to contact me. I didn't even know he was coming to Berlin." The second sentence was true.

"So you're denying that you and Doctor Tretter were having an affair?" the first man said with a voice sharp as a knife.

She blushed and cast her eyes downward.

"Look at me when you answer." The command came and she whipped up her head.

"I..." she whispered, widening her eyes as she held the officer's gaze before continuing, "When I was working at Ravensbrück...I admired the Doctor's work and..." She blushed more, biting her lips. "...we engaged in a short affair." She smoothed her skirt. "But it ended when I was transferred back to Berlin. It actually was a relief for both of us, because we knew it was wrong. He was my superior." She shed a few tears for dramatic effect.

"So you haven't seen Doctor Tretter since?" the officer asked, his voice slightly less hostile.

"No." She dabbed at her eyes. "I was as surprised as anyone when Professor Scherer announced him as recipient of the professorship in internal medicine a week ago."

"Did you speak to him on that day?" he insisted.

Anna barely suppressed a shiver and instead faked a smile. "Only a few minutes. He was so happy. This was such an accomplishment; you can't imagine how hard he worked to be worthy of this position."

"And did he ask you to sleep with him again?"

The question took her by surprise. "Officer! It would have been very improper, and neither of us wanted to endanger our future work relationship with the complications of an illicit affair. We both wanted to pour all our energy into the war effort."

The officer raised a brow. "Is that so?"

"Yes. Professor Scherer always says that we have to make sacrifices for the greater good." Anna held the officer's glance until she felt his determination soften.

The two officers exchanged a look and then he said, "Well. That will be enough for now."

"Thank you." Anna stood and walked towards the door. On an impulse she turned and looked at them. "I hope you find him."

"We will, Fräulein, we will."

Anna prayed they were wrong.

CHAPTER 30

T hat evening when Peter picked her up from work, he didn't pull her in for a much-needed hug and kiss, but told her to meet him at her place in five.

"Peter, what's wrong?" she asked, worried, when she unlocked the door.

"Nothing, sweetheart, but I think it's best if we lie low for a while. We don't want to raise any suspicions." Only when she'd locked the door after they both slipped through did he wrap her up in his arms. "How was your day?"

"The Gestapo came and questioned everyone." Anna leaned her head against his chest, and sensed the stumble in his heartbeat at the mention of the Gestapo.

"And?" He held her at arm's length, looking into her eyes.

"They believed my story. But..." Bile rose in her throat and she willed it down. "...They knew about...him and me... so I told them we had engaged in a short affair that ended when I moved back to Berlin."

"Good, that's believable enough." The pained expression

on his face belied his words. She knew he hated what had happened to her.

"I'm free now. He's gone," Anna said. The guilt over killing a man, even if that man had been a monster, tarnished her soul. But bit by bit she was coming to terms with the consequences of her actions. "Professor Scherer is very upset about the doctor's disappearance."

"I don't know why. In the circle he travels in, people go missing all the time," Peter said. "Don't worry. They'll never find a trace."

Anna wanted to ask Peter about the body, but she didn't. Some things were best kept a secret.

Weeks went by, and Anna stopped looking over her shoulder and jumping every time she heard boots clicking on the floor. As Peter had promised, the Gestapo never found Doctor Tretter's body and soon the furor over his disappearance became nothing but a distant memory.

She and Peter were done with hiding their relationship, and with a hammering heart she took him to meet her mother and Ursula. Much to Anna's relief, they accepted him into their hearts even after the couple revealed that Peter was not his real name.

Anna continued to inject the children and prisoners with saline solution, but in the general tension awaiting the Allied invasion in France, no one seemed to notice that none of them were getting sick. Perhaps they took it as a sign that the vaccine worked, but before Anna was tasked with writing a concluding report, another catastrophe struck the research team at the Charité.

The remaining male staff members below the age of forty were conscripted, and with the resources spread too thin, Professor Scherer had to announce that the entire roster of research activities would be moved to another location. Employees with a medical background were offered jobs in the hospital part of the Charité, while administrative staff was assigned to work in ammunition factories. Anna was called into the professor's office.

"Fräulein Klausen," the professor said, "it would be a shame to waste your brilliance working as a nurse. Therefore, I have pulled a few strings with old friends, and there may be an opportunity for you to continue your scientific work under another superior, should you decide to accept the position."

"That is very considerate of you," Anna said, eager to hear more about the opportunity.

"Since all research regarding bacterial infection and diseases is going to the camp in Auschwitz, the head physician Doctor Mengele has agreed to take over two persons from my staff to continue the experiments under his lead." Professor Scherer looked at her expectantly.

Anna had worked long in enough in Ravensbrück to know that Auschwitz was the *ultimate destination* for the Jews. Even though she had no idea what exactly happened there, she knew without the shadow of a doubt that she didn't want to set foot in it.

"Auschwitz, that's an awfully long way from here," she said to gain time. She didn't want the professor to think she was ungrateful for his efforts, but she would never let herself be an accomplice in the Nazis' crimes again.

"I would hate to lose you to Doctor Mengele, but I won't stand in your way if you wanted to pursue this opportunity. It may be the chance of your lifetime, Fräulein

Klausen," the professor said, with a sad expression on his face.

"Professor Scherer, thank you for the offer, but I would rather stay near my mother and my sister than work somewhere far away in the East," Anna said. Even though her career lay in tatters, relief flowed over her. Ursula had been right all along. Building a career on top of the suffering of others wasn't worth it. She would be a lot happier working as a simple nurse who healed people instead of making them suffer.

"Go home for the evening. There's nothing else for you to do. Tomorrow, please report at the hospital administration to be assigned a job as nurse." Professor Scherer walked her to the door and then he smiled, saying, "I'm happy you'll be staying here."

"Me too."

Anna had a skip in her step when she walked to the small bakery where she'd agreed to meet Peter. He'd be so happy about her good news.

CHAPTER 31

P eter stood up when he saw her coming towards him, a
smile on his tense face. Anna squinted her eyes at him,
praying that he didn't bear bad news. After their recent
scare, she'd become so accustomed to reading every one of
his expressions – and probably reading too much into them.

"Sweetheart." He wrapped his arms around her and
kissed her lightly on the lips before he pulled out the chair
for her. "What do you want to eat?"

"What do they have?" She let her eyes travel across the
meager contents of the show window. She spied a brioche
braid and pointed at it. "The *Hefezopf* looks good."

Minutes later Peter returned to their small table in the
corner of the bakery with two mugs of *Ersatzkaffee*, and a
plate with two pieces of *Hefezopf*. Anna raised a brow as he
almost spilled the coffee when setting it down. *Why is he so
nervous? The Tretter incident is long forgotten.*

"I need to tell you something," he said as he took a seat
beside her.

Anna nodded, a lump forming in her throat. Judging by the expression on his face she wouldn't like his impending confession.

"It's...I thought...there are still some things you don't know about me," he said, impaling a piece of brioche with his fork.

Fear grabbed at Anna's heart. "Go on."

He glanced around to make sure nobody was eavesdropping, and lowered his voice. "Please hear me out first? I didn't tell you earlier, because..." He rubbed his beard. "...because I didn't know how. But I don't want any secrets between us, when..." He paused and glanced at her.

"You're scaring me, Peter," Anna whispered.

"It's nothing to be scared of, it's just..." He put a hand on hers as if to make sure she wouldn't run away, took a deep breath, and then said, "I told you that after finishing school I'd had enough of the countryside and moved to Warsaw where I joined the Polish Army. But that wasn't the only reason. I had met a girl during the summer and when she became pregnant we married, and I moved to Warsaw to live with her family."

"You're married?" Anna gasped and put a hand over her mouth.

"No. I'm widowed and..." His voice broke and now it was Anna who held onto his hand to make sure he wouldn't run away.

"What happened?" she asked, her heart breaking for him.

"Her family...she...they were Jews. A few months before Hitler invaded, I sent Ludmila, our son Janusz, and Ludmila's sister to live with my family on the farm, because I thought they would be safer there than alone in the capital."

He gazed at Anna with a sadness in his eyes she'd never seen before. "I never saw them again. After my escape to Britain, I received notice that all three had been interned in the Lodz Ghetto."

"Lodz?" Anna hadn't heard that name before.

"It's been renamed Litzmannstadt after the invasion," Peter explained and then continued. "A year later the British intelligence service found out that Ludmila had died in Lodz and Jan had been on one of the transports to the camp in Chelmno."

Anna shuddered. Chelmno was high in the hierarchy of concentration camps, one of six camps located in occupied Poland designed as an ultimate destination for Jews. An orphaned child on its own had zero chance of surviving even a single week. "How old was your son?"

"Eight or nine." Peter's eyes became damp.

"I'm so sorry," Anna said and busied herself with her brioche. So much grief in the world caused by a single man's madness. A long silence ensued between them, where both of them were lost in thought.

"Anna." His voice cut through her reflectiveness. "This part of my life is long over. But I wanted you to know about it, because I want to move forward, with you." He gave her a nervous smile and made her stand up, before he bent on one knee and said, "Anna Klausen, I love you with all my heart. Will you marry me? Be my partner through these bad times and the good ones that will follow? Have my children? Be my helpmate in all areas of our lives?"

Anna wept tears of joy by the time he finished speaking, and couldn't summon her voice to answer him. She nodded and then found herself scooped into his arms as he kissed her soundly right there in the back of the bakery. When he released her, the other patrons, mostly women, were clapping their hands and smiling at them.

"I will. I will. I'd never want to live a single day without you," Anna declared, finding her voice again. Peter grinned at her with so much joy it swept her away.

"It's not gold, but it's a ring." He chuckled as he pushed an antique silver ring with a blue stone on her finger.

"I love it because it's a gift from you." Anna kissed him and they left the bakery hand in hand. They caught the bus to her family's place to tell Mutter and Ursula about the engagement.

"Anna, Peter, come in." Mutter greeted them with a tired face. She had recently been forced to take up work in an ammunition factory.

"Mutter, you look exhausted, are you alright?" Anna asked as they moved into the kitchen, where she stopped short at the sight of a tall, honey-blonde, and very thin woman about her age.

"This is Sabine," Mutter said, introducing them, "our bombed-out refugee. And this is my second daughter, Anna, and her boyfriend, Peter."

Anna disliked the woman at first glance, but made an effort not to show it and gave her a friendly smile. "Nice to meet you."

"The same to you," Sabine answered and extended her hand to shake first hers, and then Peter's. But not before giving them a once-over from head to toe.

"Where's Ursula?" Anna asked her mother.

"Queuing for rations," Mutter said, shrugging, "poor girl. So far along, and now the entire household rests on her shoulders. I would rather see her safe in the country with Lydia, but she insists that she's needed here."

Sabine perked up her ears, and Anna felt the hair on her neck stand on end.

"Frau Klausen," Peter said, squeezing Anna's hand. "In the absence of your husband, I would like to ask you for your daughter's hand."

Mutter plopped down on the kitchen chair and stared at both of them, and then she started to laugh uncontrollably for such a long time that Anna became scared. She hadn't worked as nurse for quite a while, but she still knew the signs of a nervous breakdown.

"We'll take my mother to her room," she said with a side-glance at Sabine, who dutifully stepped out of the way.

When Anna closed the bedroom door behind them and Sabine was out of earshot, her mother stopped giggling and switched on the radio to a program with folks songs.

"I'm sorry. The last days have been dreadful. For the past decade the government has acknowledged the woman's role at home and hearth, has encouraged us to bear and raise children, and now that they've sent our husbands and sons to war they force us to work in their ammunition factories. What kind of world is this?" Tears rolled down Mutter's cheeks, which scared Anna even more, because she'd never seen her mother cry until this moment.

"You could get an exception from work on medical grounds," Anna said.

"No. I will work alright." Mutter squinted her eyes. "First Ursula gets pregnant from God knows whom and now you...you know that both of you will be sent to prison should anyone find out."

"We won't be able to legally marry," Peter said. He would never get the documents needed for a marriage license with his false papers. And his true identity as a Pole having a relationship with a German woman would land him in a concentration camp faster than he could spell his name.

"We don't need the Nazis' approval, but we can be married in the sight of God," Anna said.

"Don't tell me you are in a delicate condition too." Mutter glanced at Anna's stomach.

"No. No." Anna shook her head. "But I love Peter and want to be with him."

"What if I say no?" Mutter said, her eyes darting from her daughter to Peter.

Peter bowed his head, "I would of course respect your wish, Frau Klausen. But I would try to change your mind."

For a moment Anna's heart was squeezed, but then she saw her mother smile.

"Don't worry. I give you my blessing. Since none of my children will listen to me anymore, I can only hope you have more success in keeping Anna out of trouble."

"Thank you, Frau Klausen. I will most certainly try," Peter said with a chuckle.

∽

A week later Anna and Peter stood together in Pfarrer Bernau's private office. Under the current circumstances, he had agreed to wed them in an illicit ceremony, giving their relationship God's blessing.

Behind the happy couple stood Mutter with a solemn face, Ursula weeping a flood of joyful tears, and Anna's youngest sister, Lotte. When Anna phoned her the news, Lotte had moved heaven and earth to receive a travel permit to assist at her *best friend's* wedding.

"Things may seem difficult or impossible right now, but they won't stay this way. The war will end and things will change for all of us. Meanwhile I am honored to unite this man Piotr Zdanek and the woman he has chosen to become his wife, Anna Klausen. Albeit not in the name of the Government, but in the name of God, He who matters most."

They exchanged their vows and then the priest said with a twinkle in his eyes, "You may now kiss the bride."

Peter swept her up in his arms and pressed a kiss on her lips, making her heart burst with unconditional love.

EPILOGUE

T he next day, Anna and Peter accompanied Lotte to the train station. The name Alexandra felt foreign on her lips, but the more she said it, the easier it became.

"Alexandra, you can't imagine how much it meant to us that you came to our ceremony," Anna said and hugged her sister tight.

"I wouldn't want to miss my savior's happy day for anything in the world," Lotte said and then giggled. "Although I would hope that at least one of us will get a *real* wedding."

Peter raised a brow, and Anna said, "I'll explain later, darling."

"Alexandra, the train south departs over there," Anna said, heading for the other side of the station.

"Wait." Lotte tugged at her sleeve, guilt written all over her face.

"Oh, no! What have you done now?" Anna felt the ground move beneath her feet.

"Promise you won't tell Mutter for now?" Lotte begged her with huge puppy eyes.

Anna sighed, but nodded.

"I'm going East. Alexandra Wagner, freshly baked German *Wehrmachtshelferin* and English spy, has orders to report to the military administration tomorrow morning regarding my new position as radio operator in Warsaw."

Peter's eyes widened with every word. "You can't do that. It's much too dangerous. Warsaw may seem firmly in German hands, but the Red Army is approaching and the Polish Home Army ready for a counterstrike. You'll most certainly die."

"I'd rather die trying to save what is left of my country than hide one day longer in the convent." Lotte shrugged and then she took a step towards Peter to hug him tight. "Take care of my sister, big man."

Next thing Anna knew, her baby sister had boarded a train to Warsaw.

⁓

Thank you so much for taking the time to read WAR GIRL ANNA.

If you enjoyed the book would you do me a huge favor and leave me a review? I'd really, really appreciate it.

The next book in the series is RELUCTANT INFORMER.

The Klausen's new roommate Sabine Mahler receives an *offer* from the Gestapo, she cannot refuse.

In her quest to save her husband's life, is she willing to surrender Ursula and her mother to them?

Find out here: Reluctant Informer

Sign up to my newsletter to be the first one to know when a new book is released. As a subscriber you'll be able to download my free short story DOWNED OVER GERMANY, which tells you Tom Westlake's story, before he met Ursula and fell in love with her.

http://kummerow.info/newsletter-2

AUTHOR'S NOTES

Dear Reader,

Thank you so much for reading WAR GIRL ANNA.

At the end of War Girl Lotte, Anna was left in a predicament, but I knew she would somehow find a way out.

Writing Anna's book was very challenging at times, because she had to endure so much. I must confess that at times I hated her a bit for being so weak and not resisting more openly, but in the end she found her moral compass and acted accordingly.

And Peter, don't get me started about him. I loved him from the first moment he appeared in the story. The character of Peter was inspired by my visit to the Warsaw Uprising Museum. He'll definitely get his own book, because I want to write about those incredibly brave and courageous Poles, fighting for their freedom.

As you know I like to incorporate true events into my stories and have sprinkled the names of famous persons from the forties into the story. Professor Scherer is a fictional person, but there really was a doctor called Georg Bessau at the Charité. He was the head physician of the pediatrics clinic and responsible for carrying out excruciating tuberculosis vaccination experiments on handicapped children who often died after long periods of suffering.

The Schwanenwerder Island already featured in my book Unyielding, and in my research I found out that apart from Goebbels and other high-society Nazis, there lived only one ordinary family on the island. The Schertz family owned the smallest house on Schwanenwerder. And here's the interesting fact: Mr. Schertz had been dismissed from his job as police officer because he belonged to the free masons. Nevertheless little Georg played often with Helmut Goebbels – the only boy in the same age on the exclusive island.

Apparently Joseph and Magda Goebbels were more worried that their son would become too "feminine" playing with his five sisters, than they were of letting him play with the son of a Freemason.

Many thanks go as usual to my fantastic cover designer Daniela Colleo from stunningbookcovers.com who has been ever patient with my constant tweaks and changes to have the perfect cover.

Tami Stark, my editor, and Martin O'Hearn my proofreader make sure this book the best it can be and clean up typos, unclear sentences, or anachronistic terms.

More thanks go to JJ Toner, an author of Second World War Fiction himself who generously offered to beta-read War Girl Anna. He's one of the best proofreaders around, except for his insistence to use British English as opposed to American English

Jaroslaw Pacewicz, a former colleague of mine has helped me with translations into Polish.

But my biggest thanks goes out to all the wonderful readers in the Second World War Club Facebook group, for their constant support and valuable input. I love you!

If you're seeking a group of wonderful people who have an interest in WW2 fiction, you are more than welcome to join our group.

https://www.facebook.com/groups/962085267205417

Again, I want to thank you from the bottom of my heart for taking the time to read my book and if you liked it (or even if you didn't) I would appreciate a sincere review.

Last but not least I want to thank my family for not letting me become a hermit, holed up in my writing cave day and night.

Marion Kummerow

From the Ashes (Book 1)

On the Brink (Book 2)

Historical Romance

Second Chance at First Love

Find all my books here:

http://www.kummerow.info

CONTACT ME

I truly appreciate you taking the time to read (and enjoy) my books. And I'd be thrilled to hear from you!
If you'd like to get in touch with me you can do so via

Twitter:
http://twitter.com/MarionKummerow

Facebook:
http://www.facebook.com/AutorinKummerow

Website
http://www.kummerow.info

Made in United States
North Haven, CT
13 January 2024

47409886R00126